skipping across the RUBICON

MARTIN SEIBEL

abbott press

The lyrics to "Sweet Leilani" are used with the permission of the copyright holder, Royal Music Publisher; words and music by Harry Owen, copyright 1937; all rights reserved and used by permission.

Abbott Press books may be ordered through booksellers or by contacting:

Abbott Press
1663 Liberty Drive
Bloomington, IN 47403
www.abbottpress.com
Phone: 1 (866) 697-5310

Because of the dynamic nature of the Internet, any web addresses or links contained in this book may have changed since publication and may no longer be valid. The views expressed in this work are solely those of the author and do not necessarily reflect the views of the publisher, and the publisher hereby disclaims any responsibility for them.

Any people depicted in stock imagery provided by Thinkstock are models, and such images are being used for illustrative purposes only. Certain stock imagery © Thinkstock.

ISBN: 978-1-4582-1885-8 (sc)
ISBN: 978-1-4582-1886-5 (hc)
ISBN: 978-1-4582-1887-2 (e)

Library of Congress Control Number: 2015904116

Print information available on the last page.

Abbott Press rev. date: 06/11/2015

dedication

This book is dedicated to my wife of long standing, Beverly Kirby Seibel, my muse, primary editor, and art director whose insistence (read nagging) prompted me to write this, my first novel

chapter 1

A S THE CROW FLIES, AMBERFIELDS, the latest in "Adult Community Living", lies twenty miles southwest of Summit City. But driving there along County Route 217 as it winds through the rural countryside it's some thirty miles. Heading there in the backseat of his son Robert's SUV, Maxfield Porter felt uncomfortable. The SUV rode hard and stiff like a truck, and unlike Max's Buick, its seat wouldn't conform to his backside. Even the seatbelt, which was cinched as tight as it would go, did not keep him from rolling awkwardly from side to side as the SUV negotiated the winding county road.

But it wasn't just the SUV that caused his discomfort. Max was a longtime resident of Summit City, a pillar of the community, a Summit City committeeman, and a friend to his neighbors and neighborhood, and now at only sixty-nine he felt he had lost control of his life. Others had stronger arguments in the determination of his future. Those things that made him feel comfortable and fulfilled were no longer considered important. The personal security of home and friends offered little compared to the safety and planned living of the everything-done-for-you megacommunity. He became depressed thinking of no longer having to mow the lawn or take the garbage cans out to the curb or paint the front door—all the things one does because it's the responsibility of ownership and therefore its pride.

Ever since his son and daughter-in-law broached the subject of his moving to an adult community, Max had felt a change wash over him. At the mere mention of *senior citizen*, he became defensive and found it difficult if not impossible to maintain his amiability, a quality that had endeared Max to all who knew him. His once-famous sense of humor seemed lost, and his voice became sharp and waspish. "I don't know why we couldn't take my car. It's a lot more comfortable than this tank of yours. I still don't understand why you need an SUV. I'll bet you've never even had it in four-wheel drive." The comments were so unlike him, and they elicited no response from the front seat.

Max looked over the back of the driver's seat at his son and saw how tensely he held the wheel. *Why is Robert so uptight?* he wondered. *Didn't I agree to take a look at the place?*

Robert, white-knuckled and silent, drove on.

Max turned and looked at his daughter-in-law. She was facing forward, searching for the turnoff. Sitting directly behind her, Max saw only the back of her head, her mannish cropped auburn hair, drop earrings, and thin neck. The view reminded him of the back-of-the-head photographs in *Fahrenheit 451*. He stifled a laugh and instead asked, "How did you find this place, Jeanne?"

Jeanne swiveled around to face him. Max was conscious of her close-set green eyes and pinched mouth that combined to make an otherwise attractive woman look hard and unforgiving. "A co-worker recommended it. Her uncle took an apartment here, and he couldn't be happier. He says the facilities are great, and the service is superb. Everything is taken care of for you. It's like living on a cruise ship. You won't have to worry about a thing. You'll love it."

Max wondered how she could be so sure he would love it. He had made his feelings about cruises known often enough. He hated them! And that remark about everything being taken care of was another one of her references to his house. Jeanne would never let go. Nor would she ever understand. How could she? To her, nothing was as important as moving forward. Anything that impeded her mobility was an obstacle to her career goals. That's why she and Robert lived in an apartment. No house for her no matter how much Robert wanted one.

But Max's house represented the happiest, most productive years of his life. It was where he and Dorothy had shared each other, where they had planned their business, and—with a second mortgage—they had gotten the money to start it. With Dorothy gone these past seven years and the business sold, he cherished the house and the memories that lived there with him.

They drove on in silence, Robert wishing it were all over, Jeanne hoping that her father-in-law would see things her way, and Max wondering what he was getting himself into.

The first Max had heard of Amberfields had been the month before when Jeanne had handed him a brochure. "What's this?" he had asked.

It was Robert who answered, "Well, Dad, it's a place you might want to look at."

"Why?" Max became defensive. He wondered what they were cooking up.

"Jeanne and I are concerned about your living alone in this big house."

Jeanne took over. "All these rooms for just one person. The upkeep alone must be a considerable drain on your resources. You certainly don't want to spend your retirement tied down to this barn of a house."

Jeanne saw the muscles in Max's face tighten and realized that calling his house a barn was a mistake. She had jumped in too soon. She switched to damage control. "It *is* such a lovely house. You must have wonderful memories, but don't you think the memories will stay with you no matter where you live?"

"Yes, they will," Max admitted. "But it's a lot more than that, Jeanne. I'm comfortable here. In my disorganized way, I know where I am, and I know where everything is. And all my friends are close by."

"But you are alone most of the time. Suppose something happened?" Robert asked.

"You talk as though I were ancient. Damn it! I'm not yet seventy! I look and feel more like fifty-five! I have all my faculties, and I can keep up with guys a lot younger. I don't see myself spending the remainder

3

of my life playing bingo or taking senior citizen bus excursions to the casinos. So if this brochure is about a retirement home, senior citizen village, or whatever they call these warehouses now, I'm not interested! Try me in ten years. I'll look at your brochure then."

But a week later, Max did look at the brochure. He had gone to dinner with Robert and Jeanne, and the subject came up again. Jeanne subtly worked it into the conversation. "I drove past your house yesterday on my way to a client's office. I noticed you've done a little fixing up."

"Just some paint on the window frames," Max replied.

"Why didn't you call me, Dad? I would have given you a hand," Robert said.

"No need, son. You have enough to do. I had plenty of help. My friends pitched in."

Jeanne, quick to score a point, put in, "You're lucky to have friends willing to help out like that. Those little jobs can be costly."

"Well, you have to look at it from the perspective of a bunch of retired guys who are always looking for something productive to do. As for the cost, there were some brushes, paint, masking tape, and some beer and hamburger money. It didn't add up to much considering the good time we had. And the job got done! I'd still be waiting if I called in a contractor."

Robert spoke up, "Dad, how much does it cost to keep up the house? You know, taxes, heating, electricity, maintenance. Did you ever sit down and figure out what it really amounts to?"

Max felt the old argument creeping up on him. He went on the offensive. "What difference does it make how much it costs me? I can afford it. And there'll still be plenty left for you when I—"

Robert cut him off. "You know that's not what this is all about! We worry about you being alone. Working the hours we do, we can't spend as much time with you as we would like. And don't tell us that we shouldn't worry about you, that you're a big boy now and you can take care of yourself. Remember what you told me when I was growing up? You said it's important to care about people. Well, Dad, I care about you. I may not have told you often enough, but I love you, so don't hand me the old argument that I don't have to worry about you. If you fell off a ladder or tripped down the cellar stairs, there wouldn't be anyone to help you. Your buddies aren't around all the time. And since you seldom recharge your cell phone battery, you couldn't even call for help!"

Robert ran out of steam, and a heavy silence settled about the table as he caught his breath. For the first time in their marriage, Jeanne was out of the loop. She was afraid that Max would storm out of the restaurant and that would be the end of that. On the other hand, she had never heard Robert speak so passionately. If Max wouldn't listen to logical arguments, would his son's emotional outburst persuade him?

Robert's moist eyes fixed on his father's face. He expected an explosive response, but instead Max sat back in his chair, his face softening into a smile that widened into a grin. He reached out and put his hand on Robert's shoulder and squeezed. "I've waited a long time to hear you speak up for yourself, son. If it means that much to you, we'll take a look at that place. In the meantime, let's order. I'm starved!"

chapter 2

"THERE IT IS," JEANNE SAID, pointing to the hunter green sign with *Amberfields* spelled out in raised gold letters. A smaller sign indicated that this was the visitors' entrance. Robert slowed and turned into the entrance drive. Twenty yards farther brought them to a rather elaborate gatehouse. A uniformed guard stood beside the gatehouse door with a clipboard in his hand. "Good afternoon. May I have your name please?" he asked.

"Mr. Max Porter and family," Robert reported. "We're here to see Mrs. Simmons."

The guard raised his clipboard and surveyed its contents. Finding Max's name, he checked it off. "Please continue to the administration building. Visitor parking is to the right of the main entrance. A receptionist will direct you from there." He reached in through the open gatehouse door and pressed a button. The barrier opened, and with a casual salute, he waved them on.

As they drove toward the administration building Jeanne asked excitedly, "Can we drive around first and look at the facilities and grounds before we see Mrs. Simmons?"

Max was impatient. He wanted to get on with it. "No, I think we'll head straight to Mrs. Simmons," he countered.

Jeanne's response was silence and a well hidden pout.

Looking through the SUV's window as they drove, Max had glimpses of the lake, the golf course, the clubhouse, and the gym. Through the opposite window the townhouses spread to what looked like infinity. He estimated that Amberfields consumed more than a hundred acres, almost a small town. It was more than enough to swallow up Max Porter.

Robert drove straight ahead to the administration building and pulled into a visitor's space. As they walked up the five marble steps to the imposing main entrance, Max noticed a number of electric vehicles parked to the left of the steps. They looked like golf carts but were large enough to carry six to eight passengers. Max intuited what they were used for. "It looks like we're going to have the grand tour you wanted, Jeanne."

The lobby was sizeable and pretentious. Directly in the center was a large architectural model of the Amberfields campus. Approaching it, Max could now see Amberfields in proper perspective. He traced their route from the entrance gate and got a better sense of what he had seen from the car window. He also saw what couldn't be seen from the car—another golf course and a smaller lake marked "Lower Lake" on the model and the sprawling, five-story apartment complex. Beyond the second golf course was an area of unattached single-family homes. Max read the brass plate attached to the display and smiled when he saw that his estimate of Amberfields's area was off by only one and three-tenths of an acre. He also noticed that Jeanne was getting impatient. He shepherded Jeanne and Robert to reception, where Max announced his appointment with Mrs. Simmons. The coolly efficient receptionist murmured into an intercom, and soon a smartly dressed young woman appeared and introduced herself as Carol, Mrs. Simmons's secretary. "Mrs. Simmons sends her apologies. Her prior appointment has run a little longer than expected. She suggests that you might like to take the tour now and have your meeting when you get back. I'll arrange for Sarah, one of our sales associates, to accompany you. She's very knowledgeable and can answer any questions you may have."

Max had no objections. He preferred to be outside in the sunshine rather than inside waiting for Mrs. Simmons. Carol led them outside to one of the waiting electric carts. After she introduced Sarah and thanked Max for his understanding and patience, Carol beat a hasty retreat back to Mrs. Simmons's office.

The tour was informative, and Sarah was a delightful guide who was able to mix information with humor. Within minutes, she learned that Max was a widower and unattached, so she let him know he didn't qualify for the single-family homes, which were available only to couples. The tour continued to the town houses. Max voiced his dislike of town houses. In his opinion they were fire traps.

"I think you'd be more comfortable with a one or two bedroom accommodation in the apartment complex," Sarah ventured. "The building is completely fireproof, and it has indoor parking, elevators, and its own dining room that some say is equal to a five-star restaurant."

"A five-room house would be more to my liking," Max responded, "but as I understand it, I would have to get married to qualify. Since there's little chance of that happening, we'd better look at the apartments."

On the way to the apartment complex they toured the club-house, hobby house, and little theater, all of which Max viewed unenthusiastically.

All through the tour Jeanne had effusively commented on the facilities. Everything was perfect, she declared. Robert, on the other hand, made few comments. In fact, he was concerned about his father's attitude. Max seemed almost indifferent, not at all what he thought his father's reaction would be. He was afraid that Max had resigned himself to an unwelcome fate, and that was the last thing Robert wanted.

"Impressive," Max offered as they entered the lobby of the apartment complex. He turned to his daughter-in-law. "If the dining room is as good as they claim, this could very well be the cruise ship you mentioned, Jeanne."

Sarah was puzzled. "Cruise ship?" she questioned.

"My daughter-in-law feels that living here would be like living on a cruise ship ... just one long vacation. Now let's see those apartments."

chapter 3

MRS. SIMMONS'S OFFICE WAS TASTEFULLY appointed. Three walls displayed color photographs and architectural renderings of the various buildings, homes, and facilities that comprised Amberfields. The fourth wall contained a bank of windows that looked out on the upper lake. In front of the windows a sofa, coffee table, and two chairs formed a conversation center. On the other side of the room was a highly polished rosewood desk. The chairs facing the desk were high-backed and covered with supple rosewood-colored leather. Mrs. Simmons showed the three Porters to these chairs and then seated herself behind her desk. She wore a chocolate brown pants suit with matching leather pumps and a light yellow blouse. Her blonde hair hung loosely yet perfectly about her shoulders. Everything about the office, including Mrs. Simmons, was aesthetically pleasing.

"I hope you enjoyed your tour of Amberfields and all it has to offer our member owners." Mrs. Simmons spoke directly to Max, looking for some reaction. According to Sarah, Max had asked the right questions but, she felt, without enthusiasm. Was it Amberfields? Was it the price? Or did Max Porter just want to stay where he was? Mrs. Simmons wished he would give her a clue so she could tailor her sales pitch. She got up from her chair, walked around to the front, and leaned against the edge of the desk in front of Max. "Sarah told me of your interest in the two-bedroom apartment in the north wing."

She's good, Max thought. *She's going to work on me.* "Well," he replied, "it wouldn't make sense to leave a perfectly good house in a perfectly good neighborhood and trade it for another house or one of those town houses. No, if I'm going to make the change, it will be into an apartment. Two bedrooms would be just right, one to sleep in and the other for my books and things, a library or study of sorts, a gym for my mind so that my brain muscle doesn't atrophy."

Max had made up his mind. In fact, he had made up his mind halfway through the tour. After that night at the restaurant he knew that he would have to leave his house. It was for the best now that he understood Robert's concerns. Yet deep down he still had the feeling that, like an old and useless Eskimo, he was being put out on an ice floe to wither and die, thereby unburdening the tribe. *No matter*, Max thought. *It has to be done.* And so to the satisfaction of everyone except himself, he said, "I think, Mrs. Simmons, it's time to get down to business!"

It took an hour for Max to work out the details with Mrs. Simmons, sign papers, and pay a deposit. As soon as his lawyer approved the contract, Max would become an official member owner of a two-bedroom apartment in the north wing of the apartment complex at Amberfields. After she shook Max's hand and offered congratulations, Mrs. Simmons walked with the Porters to the main entrance, still extolling the advantages of Amberfields. After a final good-bye she returned to her office, and the Porters walked toward their car. Robert felt relieved that it was all over. Jeanne reveled in once again having gotten her way, and Max again wondered what he had gotten himself into.

As he was getting into the car, Max noticed one of the electric carts pull up and discharge its passengers. The guide was helping a rather stout woman to alight from the cart. She was accompanied by a very attractive younger woman and a teenage girl. Max paused at the open car door, looking at the three women. A cloud of doubt formed around his head. He wondered if his life was now to be filled with overweight old ladies. He shook off the thought and got into the car.

chapter 4

A MONTH LATER AFTER HE had sold his house, settled his affairs, and hardest of all, said his good-byes, Max was established in his apartment. The transition from a twelve-room house to a two-bedroom apartment was not an easy one. Max had realized that most of his furniture would have to go, as would many of his possessions. He picked out the barest minimum of furniture for his new apartment and sold or gave away most of the rest. His possessions required more thought. As most people do, he had accumulated many things over the years, each with its own memory. Then there was his film collection, his long-standing hobby. Would he have to dispose of the films that had taken him more than thirty years to acquire? But why keep them, he thought, if he was unable to show them? He put them into storage along with the remaining furniture. He would need time to sort things out.

Although he hadn't actually measured, Max was certain that the entire apartment would have fitted into the living room and dining room of his old house. When he first saw it, the apartment was empty and undecorated, and with its white walls it looked spacious. Now decorated and furnished, it looked cluttered and cramped. Part of the reason was the furniture. As little as he had brought with him, it was too much for the smaller space. He had allowed Jeanne to do the decorating, which turned out to be a disaster. She leaned toward dark, heavy colors that had the effect of pulling in the walls and robbing the apartment of any character. It was neither masculine nor feminine but rather commercial, much like the booths at a trade fair or a department store furniture display. He was uncomfortable, but he left the apartment as it was. He wasn't supposed to be comfortable on an ice floe.

Max spent the first week orienting himself to his new environment. He met the neighbors on either side of his apartment, nice couples who were considerably older than he was. He sensed that one of the wives, Edna Canfield, was a confirmed matchmaker. She had that look in her eye, and Max felt she was mentally matching him up with her database of eligible lady friends. Her husband, Arthur, was an inveterate golfer who spent most of his waking hours on the links or in the clubhouse.

Max signed up for the health club, visited the clubhouse, walked the grounds, and had dinner in the dining room, which he found to be excellent in both food and service. He was invited to join a number of clubs, but none interested him. He didn't turn any down but said it was too early to make a decision. No matter how agreeable the facilities were, Max still looked upon Amberfields as a drifting ice floe, carrying him away from the familiar and fulfilling life he had known.

As the weeks passed, Max settled into a routine not unlike the one he had practiced before he had moved to Amberfields, except the rhythm was different. He rose at seven instead of his usual six. At first he considered it a lost hour, sixty productive minutes dissolving into nothingness. He tried to justify it, to see it through the eyes of the people he had met in his first weeks at Amberfields, to get their take on life before and after coming to live here. It all came to the same thing. "This is retirement, time to settle back and enjoy yourself. No more being a slave to your alarm clock. No more rushing except to make your tee-time."

But it didn't work for Max. He had been retired for a number of years before he had come to Amberfields. Even in retirement his life had been full, productive, and happy. So far he couldn't find one thing in this new environment that would be worthy of a shout of *carpe diem* as he threw back the covers and jumped out of bed!

After getting up, he would start a pot of coffee, and while it brewed, he would wash and get into his exercise togs. After a quick cup of coffee he would go to the gym for an hour, and then he would spend another hour in the indoor swimming pool. After he exercised, he would return to his apartment to shower, shave, and get dressed. He wasn't a neat freak, but he enjoyed being well turned out in clean, matching clothes. Many of his friends from the old neighborhood looked like walking rummage sales, not because they couldn't afford to dress well, but after they had spent their working lives in suits and ties, it was no longer important to them. Dressing up was for lodge meetings, weddings, and funerals. After he dressed, Max would decide whether to have breakfast in his apartment or go to the dining room. This was his new morning routine.

Max was making friends, but the level of friendship was shallow. Almost everyone played golf, and Max had no interest in the game. He had tried it when he was in his thirties and found it boring. Even worse, he had found most golfers as boring as their game. Their only topic of conversation was golf, and it was no different now. Max didn't speak golf. This left pleasantries and inanities the staple of verbal exchange. *How unnecessary*, Max thought. The same could be communicated with a grunt, a nod of the head, or a finger to the forelock. What he wouldn't give for some real conversation.

There were times when Max was overcome by homesickness. Sometimes it was so overwhelming he wanted to get into his car and drive back to the old neighborhood and spend a few hours with his buddies. He just wanted to sit around, play cards, have some beer, but mostly indulge in some good old BS sessions, the kind that said nothing and meant everything. He would be restored and fulfilled, at least for a while. But he never gave in. He was afraid that if he did, he might never return to Amberfields. He couldn't do that to Robert.

Robert called almost every evening, and he and Jeanne would usually visit every other weekend. Max would show them around, introduce them to whichever of his new acquaintances they chanced to meet, and assure Robert that he was perfectly happy with Amberfields. But Robert saw through Max's glowing delivery and realized that his father wasn't as happy as he pretended to be. Nor was Robert. He had thought that when Max settled down at Amberfields, his relationship with Jeanne would also settle down and become less stressful. Instead it proved to be just the opposite. Jeanne became more involved with her job and grew even more distant.

A month passed, and one morning after his gym workout Max decided to have breakfast in the dining room. The breakfast hour was winding down, and the room was almost empty. He saw Edna Canfield sitting alone. Arthur, Max thought, was already on the links. Max and the Canfields had become good friends. Edna had a vibrant personality that made her seem much younger than the eighty-one she admitted to. She had been, Max imagined, a very pretty girl when she was young.

"Is this a private party, or can anyone join in?" Max asked.

Edna looked up, "You qualify, Max. Sit down and have some coffee."

"I'll need more than coffee. I just did two hours in the gym," Max reported. "A large stack of wheat cakes, sausage, orange juice, and some of that coffee would just about do it."

"Leave it to me," Edna said as she signaled the waiter. "Sid, see what you can do to get some breakfast for Mr. Porter. He has a mean and hungry look."

"That's a *lean* and hungry look," Max laughingly corrected and then repeated his requirements to Sid, who scurried away to the kitchen.

Max reflected on how easy it was to talk with Edna Canfield. She had qualities he appreciated. Her interests were broad. She was intelligent and had a wonderful sense of humor, but above all, she was articulate. One could talk to Edna, and she would respond—no grunts, tips of the hat, or fingers to her forelock from Edna Canfield.

Edna studied Max. After a moment she asked, "What's troubling you, Max?" Max was amazed at Edna's perceptiveness. *Does it really show that much?* he wondered.

"Nothing," he assured her.

"Come now, Max. You look like you need more than that breakfast you just ordered."

He hesitated, not certain he wanted to discuss his problems with anyone, especially his newfound friend.

"It's nothing earth-shattering, Edna." He saw the questioning look on her face and decided to plunge ahead. "Well, I just don't fit in here at Amberfields."

Surprised, Edna inquired, "What ever gave you that idea?"

"Golf, for one thing. Most of the men and a lot of women spend almost all their time playing golf. When they're not playing, they're talking about it. I'm just not a golfer. I'm invited to join in, but when I admit to not having an interest in playing, I get, 'Oh, that's too bad,' as though I have some physical or mental short circuit that explains my lack of judgment or social ineptitude or bad taste. It all seems narrow and obsessive to me."

Edna looked at Max over the rim of her coffee cup. "You're taking it much too seriously, Max. Sure, most of the members play golf, and to some it is a passion. The two golf courses and the clubhouse are a big draw in selling Amberfields. But you'll find that for every member who is passionate for golf, there are others who find golf only a pleasant pastime ... or those who, like yourself, have no interest in golf at all but still find Amberfields the perfect place to spend their retirement. They're here, Max. You just haven't found them yet." She paused as though she was considering whether to continue. Then with a "what the hell" shrug of her shoulders, she said, "But I don't think you want to find them!"

Max stiffened and started to object, but Edna pushed on, "Don't blame golf. You really don't want to be here, do you, Max? You want to be back, safe in your big house, where you can pick and choose and close out the rest just by slamming your front door. Well, you're going to have to get over it. You live at Amberfields now, and golf or no golf, there are a lot of good people here. All you have to do is get out there and mix with them. You'll be surprised how well you'll fit in."

Max was stunned. She was right, of course. He remembered when he was ten years old, his father had changed jobs, and they relocated to Summit City. Leaving his friends and starting at a new school was the end of the world for him. He sulked for weeks, but finally new friends took over as his old friends faded into memory. And, Max recalled, the world had gone on.

Edna looked at Max, waiting for him to say something, prepared for an outburst of denial. She was unprepared for his response.

"Why didn't you tell me I was acting like a ten-year-old?" he asked.

"I thought I had," Edna responded just as Sid brought Max's breakfast.

chapter 5

LATER THAT AFTERNOON MAX RETURNED to his apartment and found a voice mail from Robert. The message was short. It was a simple, "Dad, it's now 3:10. If you get back before 5:30, call me at my office." Max looked at his watch. It was 3:20. He had missed the call by ten minutes. He dialed Robert's office number.

"Good afternoon. Mr. Porter's office."

"Hello, Nancy, this is Mr. Porter returning my son's call."

"Oh yes, Mr. Porter. He's waiting for your call. I'll put you through."

"Hi, Dad, how are you?"

"Fine. What's up?"

"I'm a bachelor tonight, and I thought if you weren't busy, I'd drive out and take you to dinner. We haven't done that for a while."

"How come you're a bachelor?"

"Jeanne is attending a meeting in San Francisco. She took the seven-o'clock flight this morning. She'll be gone for a few days. It was pretty short notice, but you know Jeanne. She never lets an opportunity get away from her."

"Yes, indeed, she's a real go-getter," Max agreed.

Robert reiterated his invitation, "So how about dinner? I can pick you up around 6:30."

From the anxious tone of Robert's voice Max sensed that he had something on his mind and wanted to talk about it. If that was the case, it would be better if Robert was on his home turf. "I have an errand in town that I've been putting off," he lied. "I can drive into town now and take care of my business and then meet you later. Say around six?"

"Are you sure you want to buck the traffic? I wouldn't mind coming out to you. We could eat in the dining room. It would save you the drive."

"The drive doesn't bother me. At this time of day the traffic is all going in the opposite direction. I enjoy watching the stop and go on the other side of the road while I'm clipping along at the speed limit."

Robert laughed and said, "Okay, Dad, you win. Meet me at my apartment. I'll be there by a quarter to six. We'll decide on a restaurant then."

Max left shortly after he hung up from Robert. He had no business to attend to, but to justify his white lie, he decided to spend some time with his friend, Dave Benjamin. He hadn't seen Dave since he had moved to Amberfields, and he felt it was about time. Dave lived in an apartment behind his store; however, when Max arrived, the store was closed, and Dave was not at his apartment. Missing Dave left Max with more than an hour to kill before he met Robert. As he sat behind the steering wheel of his car, wondering how to fill the time, it occurred to him that he might go back to see his old house. He wondered if the new owners had any improvements underway or if it looked the same. He started the engine and drove to his old neighborhood.

It was a mistake! As soon as he saw the house, he was overcome with regret. He parked across the street and sat looking at the home he had given up, his white-knuckled hands wrapped tightly around the steering wheel. It was not the same house he had left a scant two months before. The lawn hadn't been mowed, and the overgrown grass, now mostly weeds, was beginning to overtake the jumble of flotsam strewn about. In the driveway a teenage boy was working on a car while three others stood around watching. Fluid that had drained from the car was cascading down the driveway to wind up in the storm drain and continue on its polluting way to the Black River.

Max was appalled. He understood that what had been done could not be undone. Yet he had to question why he had allowed himself to be manipulated into selling his house to settle in Amberfields. He kept telling himself over and over that it was for the best, but he never really believed it. That house across the street was where he belonged. But he was now committed to Amberfields, and regardless of what Edna Canfield believed, he would never fit into the senior life there.

Seeing the house put Max into an abysmal mood that he had to shake quickly. He didn't want Robert to know how he really felt about Amberfields.

chapter 6

ROBERT HAD CHOSEN A RESTAURANT two blocks from his apartment. It was a quiet place that was dimly lit and eclectically decorated. There was something for everyone. They were tucked away at a corner table, nursing a couple of bourbons. Their conversation was light, yet hidden under the pleasantries, Max was aware of a tension within his son. He had to get Robert to talk about what was bothering him. Sensing it involved Jeanne, Max asked, "How does it feel being a bachelor?"

"It's too early to tell. I've only been a bachelor since this morning after Jeanne left for the airport. I'm still running on married time. It's just for a few days, hardly long enough to get used to."

Max started to probe, "Why the short notice? Was she replacing someone who was scheduled to go but couldn't at the last moment?"

"She didn't say, and I didn't think much about it until after she left."

"And what do you think about it now?"

"What should I think?"

"You tell me, son. I get the feeling there's something bothering you and that it concerns Jeanne. You want to talk about it? That's what this dinner is all about, isn't it?"

Robert drained the contents of his glass, put it down, and looked across the table at his father, a sheepish smile on his face. "I never could fool you, could I, Dad?"

"I'd like to believe you never tried."

Robert was surprised. "Even when I talked you into looking at Amberfields?"

"I knew you were truly concerned when you made that impassioned speech. It was sincere, and it convinced me that it was my well-being you were worried about. That's really the reason I agreed to look at Amberfields, not Jeanne's cajoling. I sensed she had an agenda that included the sale of my house. Am I right so far?"

Robert didn't answer immediately. He was looking down at his empty glass, twisting it around on the table. Finally he let go of the glass, looked across the table at his father, and answered, "Yes, Dad, Jeanne did have an agenda. This San Francisco trip is part of it. It doesn't have anything to do with her company. I doubt that her boss knows anything about it. I think she went out there for a job interview."

Max didn't like what he was hearing. "What makes you think that? Maybe you should start at the beginning."

Robert started slowly as he looked back to the beginning of the problem. "I got the first inkling of something in the wind about six months ago. She was pushing harder than usual. She would come home super hyped with a briefcase full of work and stay up half the night. I was afraid she had taken on too much and was taking pills to keep up the pace she set for herself. I confronted her with my concerns, and she told me that a new position was opening up within the company and she was being considered for it. It would be another step up for her. She mentioned that two other people were also being considered, but she knew she would beat them out because she was the better producer."

"But it didn't happen."

"No, it didn't. She was passed over."

"How did she take it?"

"Surprisingly well, I thought. She chalked it up to the breaks of the game and said that next time she would win."

Max was dubious. "That doesn't sound like Jeanne, accepting defeat like that."

"You're right," Robert agreed. "Underneath she was seething. It took only twenty-four hours for her to forget all about 'the breaks of the game.' She started bringing work home again, only it wasn't company work. She was preparing her résumé. She was looking for a new job. I didn't realize it at the time, but a few weeks later she started her campaign to get you to sell your house and move into a retirement community."

"So I wouldn't be an obstacle to your going with her if she took a job that required relocation."

"She took me in completely. I really thought she was concerned about your living alone."

"Has she had any offers?"

"None you could call serious, except this last one from San Francisco."

"How did you find all this out? Did you confront her?"

Robert shook his head. "I didn't have to. Jeanne may be very efficient at her work, but she has one gigantic flaw. She has a superiority complex. She believes she's beyond making mistakes, and that makes her careless. She left a paper trail in every wastepaper basket and garbage can in the apartment. When I became concerned and, I admit, somewhat suspicious, I played detective and gleaned enough information from her jetsam to piece together what she was doing. Unfortunately you had already bought your membership in Amberfields."

"Don't let that bother you, son. I'm perfectly content at Amberfields," he lied for the second time today. "More important is what you will do if she comes back with a job offer. San Francisco is a long way from Summit City and your job."

"She would expect me to quit my job and go with her. Jeanne is a sick girl, Dad. She's an obsessive-compulsive, career-driven workaholic. In her mind she has a career. I just have a job. To Jeanne there's only one answer. *I will go with her.*"

"Would you consider leaving your position to go with her?"

"No, I couldn't. Our marriage isn't strong enough to survive that kind of sacrifice. People like Jeanne think only of getting to the top of the ladder. They seldom realize that the top is usually far above their abilities. When they do, it's too late. Then there's only one direction left, and that's down!"

"And you would be expected to pick up the pieces."

"Yes, and nothing would be left but two lost careers, a shattered wife, and having to start all over again."

"Not a happy scenario. If Jeanne does come home with an offer, how will you handle it?"

Robert thought for a moment and then shrugged his shoulders in resignation and replied to his father's question. "I'll try to talk it out. I'll tell her why I can't leave my job."

"So you've already decided not to go with her if the situation arises."

"The decision was made for me. Last Monday my boss confirmed that he had reached the mandatory retirement age and that he would be leaving at the end of the month. It wasn't official yet, but I was to move up into his spot. That would make me vice president of operations. Ten o'clock this morning it became official. There's no way I'm going to leave."

Max was delighted. "That's wonderful, Robert." Then he became serious. "I wonder what Jeanne's reaction will be."

"We'll just have to wait and see. This may all be academic. She may not come back with a job offer. But if she does, then whether she goes to San Francisco alone or stays as the wife of a company vice president will be her decision!"

Max hoped it would be that easy, but he doubted it. It was not easy for someone like Jeanne to change. Now the competition war would expand to include Robert. Jeanne would not be satisfied until she also achieved vice-president status.

The waiter observed the pause in their conversation and approached the table with menus in hand and announced the specials of the evening.

It was late when they left the restaurant and headed for Max's car. Robert was uptight about Max driving back to Amberfields alone in the dark. "You're sure you won't stay at the apartment tonight and go back in the morning? I'd feel better if you would," he said, making the offer for the third time.

"Thanks, Robert. I appreciate your concern, but I'd prefer to sleep in my own bed. I'll be fine. I know the road, and there will be hardly any traffic." That said, Max got into his Buick, started the engine, and with a wave to Robert, pulled away from the curb. After a few twists and turns, County Road 217 appeared, and Max headed west toward Amberfields.

As the miles unwound, Max reflected on his dinner with Robert. It had been an evening filled with mixed emotions—elation at Robert's promotion, anguish at the possibility of Jeanne leaving and their marriage falling apart. The more Max thought about it, the more upset he became. He doubted there was anything he could do, yet as Robert's father, he felt obligated to try to guide him. But even if he could help or offer advice, he asked himself, "Would it be the right advice?" He wasn't so sure. He looked back over his time at Amberfields and saw nothing but failed attempts and frustration at adjusting to his new life. It was hardly the track record to qualify him as an advisor.

As he drove on, Max's thoughts moved away from Robert and centered on his own problems. When he saw his house earlier in the day, it reminded him of just how much the move to Amberfields had cost him. All those years spent maintaining it so it would be a home to be proud of evidently meant nothing to the new owner. *Where is the pride now? His friends and cronies are where they've always been. Only I am somewhere else*, he thought, too afraid of seeing them again for fear of never being able to return to Amberfields.

There was so much more—his film collection, thirty years of collecting and showing films of the golden age of film to senior citizens and college students and anyone who showed an interest. Now, because of Jeanne's agenda it was all packed away in storage, destined for disposal.

The night seemed to be getting darker, or was it his mood that was slipping deeper into darkness? Perhaps he should have spent the night with Robert after all. But it didn't matter now. The entrance to Amberfields lay just ahead, and perhaps there was some truth in the saying, "It's always darkest before the dawn."

chapter 7

THEY MET BY CHANCE IN the mail room. Max had retrieved his mail and thumbed through the accumulation, tossing the junk mail into the refuse drum to be recycled into more junk mail. When he had finished, the original pile had been reduced to two pieces of mail, both bills. He looked up and saw her across the room, going through the same sorting routine. There was something familiar about her, but he couldn't dredge up where he had seen her before. She was extremely attractive, almost beautiful, he thought. She had a slim, well-proportioned figure, almost girlish, which was contradicted by the streaks of silver that ran through her dark hair. He wished he could remember where he had seen her. It would give him the opportunity of speaking to her without seeming forward.

She looked up and saw Max staring at her. He felt embarrassed and sheepishly dropped his eyes. She addressed him, "Aren't you Max Porter?"

He looked back at her. She was smiling at him, and he was no longer embarrassed. Her smile was radiant. "Why, yes, I am. But you have me at a disadvantage, Miss—" He was sorry he replied that way. It sounded straight out of a grade-B antebellum movie.

"Marion Wade," she said. "Edna Canfield pointed you out to me. According to Edna, we have something in common."

Max was overjoyed at the opportunity of entering into a conversation with this charming lady. "I can't imagine what it might be, but I look forward to finding out."

"It seems we purchased our apartments on the same day."

Then he remembered. "Why, of course, you were just coming back from your tour of the grounds as we were leaving. When did you move in?"

"Last week. I had to wait until the original owner's new accommodations were ready. It's been over two months."

Max was delighted. "I must admit that when I saw you coming back from the tour, I assumed the lady with you was the one who was interested in Amberfields, and you were the mother of the teenage girl."

Marion Wade smiled her radiant smile, and assuming a coy Southern accent, she said, "And I presume that in that statement there reposes a compliment, for which I am, sir, eternally grateful." She had turned the Southern "B" movie into *Gone with the Wind*. Max was enthralled, a beautiful woman with a sense of humor. They both laughed at the shared joke.

Marion continued in her natural voice, "The other lady is my sister-in-law, and the teenager is my niece, who, by the way, is almost thirty and working on an advanced degree in communications."

As they talked, they moved closer to each other until they were standing together beside the mail room entrance. It was then that Max noticed her wedding ring. People came and went through the entrance and saw only two residents with mail in their hands, engaged in conversation, not an unusual occurrence in the mail room.

"How do you like it here at Amberfields?" Marion asked.

"Oh, it's not bad for an ice floe," Max replied.

Marion was puzzled by his answer. "I'm afraid that you now have me at a disadvantage, Mr. Porter. You did say ice floe, did you not?"

"Yes, Amberfields is an ice floe, albeit a very posh ice floe."

Still puzzled, she asked, "Why an ice floe? Is there something I should know about Amberfields?"

"Oh, no!" he exclaimed, "There's nothing wrong with Amberfields.

It has nothing to do with anything or anyone but me. Others might regard Amberfields as a paradise, but I see it differently."

"In spite of the lack of palm trees and the soothing sound of rolling surf, I'm one who considers Amberfields to be something of a paradise."

"And Mr. Wade, does he feel the same?" inquired Max.

"Mister Wade is in an altogether different paradise. He passed away some time ago." Giving Max no time to extend condolences, she raced on. "But tell me, Mister Porter, if there's nothing wrong with Amberfields, why do you see it as a cold and barren ice floe?" Marion asked. "I don't mean to pry, but you have piqued my curiosity."

"I'm afraid it will sound silly or worse, childish, and I certainly don't want you to think of me as silly or childish, though I'm told I do sometimes act that way. If I do tell you, will you promise not to laugh?"

"Of course I won't laugh. And please don't worry about seeming silly or childish. At our age, Mr. Porter, we've earned the right to be just that whenever we want to be."

"It's hard to think of you as my age. I'm not even going to try."

"That's nice of you to say. But you were going to explain the ice floe."

"So I was. It has to do with Eskimos. You see, when an Eskimo gets old and can no longer support his position in the tribe, instead of becoming a burden, he goes out on an ice floe and drifts away to join his ancestors. To the Eskimos it's a simple solution. No fuss, no muss. For me it's not so simple. I can't get it out of my head that Amberfields is my own personal ice floe."

Marion took a moment to digest Max's explanation. "Mr. Porter, do you really believe you are no longer useful and that you are here at Amberfields to float away and join your ancestors?" Her tone was indignant, and Max wondered if she was annoyed with his reasoning.

"Perhaps the analogy is a bit fanciful," Max admitted by way of apology, "but it did seem that I was becoming a burden to my son and daughter-in-law."

"Did they tell you that you were a burden?" she asked.

"Not in so many words. My son was worried about my living alone."

"Well, all I can say is good for him. Having a son who shows concern for his father's well-being is, in this day and age, a rarity and more then most people ever have."

Once again Max was reduced to a ten-year-old being lectured by his teacher. He looked down, hoping she wouldn't notice the hangdog expression on his face. When he looked up, she was smiling. Then he smiled, and they were smiling at each other. He hardly knew what to say to her, so all he said was, "Thanks."

"Thanks for what?" she responded.

"Thanks for not laughing. Thanks for understanding and thanks for trying to knock me off my ice floe."

"That's a lot of thanks, Mr. Porter. Are you certain you haven't forgotten any?" The lilt had returned to her voice.

"Just one," replied Max. "Thanks for starting to call me Max. Old Mr. Porter is somewhere out there, looking for his ice floe."

"Since you think so highly of ice floes and cold, barren places, you deserve to have an Eskimo name. Instead of Max, I think I'll call you Nanook."

Max was overjoyed. "Nanook!" he exclaimed, "*Nanook of the North!*"

Marion was surprised. "You know of it?" she asked.

"Of course I do! *Nanook of the North* was Robert J. Flaherty's 1922 documentary about a year in the life of the Eskimo Nanook and his family. I have a print in my film collection."

"You're a film collector?" Marion asked.

"Have been for years," Max replied. "Sixteen millimeter film, VHS video, and now DVDs." Max rambled on, "I had a twenty-seat theater in the basement of my house. I put on shows for the neighborhood kids, senior citizen groups, and anyone interested in old films. It's a great hobby. The films and projectors and all the memorabilia are in storage now, but I have some of the videos and DVDs with me."

Max was delighted with Mrs. Wade's interest in classic films but he didn't want to press the issue. She might take it as his coming on too strong and turn him away. And that was the last thing he wanted to do. Instead he responded with an offer of his own.

"Now that you've given me a new name, I must reciprocate. Since you regard life at Amberfields as paradise, albeit without palm trees or soothing surf, I dub thee Leilani ... from the song "Sweet Leilani" featured in *Waikiki Wedding*, 1937, and sung by Bing Crosby."

Marion accepted it graciously. She had little choice after Nanook.

Actually she thought it quite sweet. She noticed the time on the clock above the mailboxes. "Oh my!" she exclaimed. "I'm going to be late. I'm meeting Edna Canfield for lunch."

"No men allowed, I suppose," stated Max.

"Sorry, Nanook, no men allowed. We're doing girl talk." With that, she turned and walked out of the mail room. She had gone only a few steps when she stopped and called back to Max, "By the way, Nanook. Don't forget to wipe your mukluks before you enter your igloo."

Max stood in the doorway, legs spread and arms akimbo, watching her walk toward the restaurant. "Now that's some kind of woman," he told himself. As she entered the dining room, she looked back and saw him still standing in the doorway. She smiled, and he thought she waved to him. When Max could no longer see her, he headed for his apartment, whistling "Sweet Leilani". By the time he unlocked his apartment door, the ice floe had melted, and palm trees were growing in his living room.

chapter 8

A S SHE WALKED TOWARD THE restaurant, Marion was conscious of Max following her with his eyes. Under other circumstances she would be annoyed or even offended and consider it boorish behavior, but it seemed that she enjoyed being ogled by Max Porter. From their few minutes together she felt he was someone she could trust. That in itself was unusual since she had found little to trust in the men who had passed through her life thus far.

Marion slowed her pace to afford Max extra time to enjoy her passage but made certain that her hips didn't sway too much. She didn't want Max to think she was having fun at his expense.

She was enjoying it, and she was pleased with that. Marion felt warm, contented, and very happy. If this feeling was the result of meeting Max Porter, she could be on the threshold of something wonderful.

When she reached the entrance to the restaurant, she turned her head and looked back toward the mail room. Max was still standing as she had left him, feet spread, hands on hips, and a broad grin on his face. She smiled back at him and raised her hand slightly as though to wave and then turned and entered the restaurant.

Edna was waiting for her, and when she saw the smile on Marion's face as she approached, she anticipated an interesting luncheon. "Good morning. Sit down and tell me all about it."

Feigning surprise, Marion looked at Edna and asked, "About what?"

"Whatever it was that gave you that glow. You floated in here like a schoolgirl who was just pinned by the star quarterback."

Marion tried to change the subject. She especially didn't want Max Porter to be the topic of conversation. "Do they still do that? I thought that went out in the fifties."

"Do what?" Edna questioned.

"Get pinned. Wasn't that what we were talking about?"

"Marion Wade, you are exasperating. Just answer one question. Did you by any chance meet Max Porter?"

"As a matter of fact, I did. We had a nice conversation."

"How did you find him?"

"That's two questions."

"Okay, answer the question, and I promise to drop the subject. Then we'll order lunch. How did you find him?"

"Interesting. I found him very interesting." With that, she signaled the waiter.

chapter 9

A FTER MARION LEFT HIM FOR her luncheon date with Edna Canfield, Max went for a walk. A long walk was in order. It offered him time to think, and he wanted to think about Marion Wade ... and Amberfields. He now found it difficult to separate the two. One seemed dependent on the other. He had barely tolerated Amberfields. But now Marion Wade had arrived, and in their five-minute meeting everything had changed. Max forgot about his dislike of Amberfields and realized that in the short space of five minutes she had melted his ice floe and made him feel comfortable, something he hadn't felt since he had come to Amberfields.

But it was more than comfort. He closed his eyes, and she was there smiling her radiant smile that so captivated him. He heard her voice, so pleasant it was almost a song. Maxfield Porter could do no more than ask himself why he felt this way. He tried to analyze his feelings, to see them in a logical pattern and understand them. These were the same feelings he had felt for Dorothy when they had first met. Now they were reborn. Had he already fallen in love with Marion Wade? Did things like that really happen? He walked on.

They were neighbors now, and he knew he would see her again. But he wanted more than just chance meetings in the mail room or dining room. He didn't want to seem aggressive. Nor did he want her to misunderstand his intentions. He knew that some unattached women were wary of men who came on too strongly. He certainly didn't want to give her the wrong impression. It was important because what he was beginning to feel for Marion transcended the physical.

Max walked toward the lake. The paved stone path was bordered by flower beds. Suddenly he stooped and picked up a stone lying among the flowers. He inspected it. It was the right size and shape. He shook off the soil that clung to it and put it in his jacket pocket. By the time he reached the lake, his pocket was bulging with similar stones. He stood at the water's edge, lost in thought. *I met her just a few minutes ago. Is it possible to feel this way about someone I've just met?* He reached into his pocket and brought out a stone. As he held it between his thumb and middle finger with his index finger positioned tightly against its thin edge, he bent his body slightly to the right, drew his arm back, and with a sidearm motion, flung the stone out over the lake. It spun in a low trajectory inches above the water. When it touched the surface, it skipped, came down, and skipped two more times before it lost its momentum and sank below the surface. *We were together only five minutes.* He took another stone and flung it across the water. *But in those five minutes I felt relaxed enough with her to tell her why I was at Amberfields and why I felt like an old Eskimo. Now I want her to know that I no longer feel that way.* Another stone, another three hops. *Should I wait for another chance meeting?* This time the stone skipped across the water four times. *No, I can't leave this to chance.* He reached into his pocket and removed the last stone. *But how can I arrange to meet her again without seeming aggressive?* He looked at the stone in his hand as though it had some mystical power. Then he reared back and flung it across the water. By the time the stone had skipped and dived below the surface, he had a plan worked out.

Max got his car and drove to Summit City. As he drove, he thought of Dorothy on the last night of her life. He remembered sitting beside her bed in that cold, impersonal hospital room. He sensed rather than heard the hiss of the oxygen as it surged through the tube fitted to her nostrils. She was bound by so many tubes, wires, sensors—the paraphernalia connecting her to the little that remained of her life. It was so useless, but it was all that could be done because there was neither the medicine nor the knowledge to cure her.

Max held her limp hand in his. He cried, tears welling in his eyes that ran down his cheeks and dripped from his chin. He was unashamed. There is no graceful way for lovers to part. Dorothy opened her eyes and looked up at him. A faint smile, recognizable only by Max, crossed her lips. She withdrew her hand from his, and straining to control it, she raised it to his face to blot his tears. It was too much of a physical strain and her hand fell. Max cradled it in his.

She was using up her strength. Every motion, every breath diminished what little was left of her life force. Her lips quivered, and Max realized she wanted to say something. He lowered his head and placed his ear close to her mouth. With great effort, slowly, painfully, Dorothy whispered, "In the drawer of the nightstand ... a letter ... for you."

Max found the letter. He opened it with trembling hands, and through glazed eyes he read,

My darling,

Ever since I learned that my cancer was inoperable and that I was going to leave you, I have searched for a way to tell you how happy you have made me. The thought of leaving you and Robert and the pain it will cause you saddens me. But pain eventually diminishes and leaves. Life goes on. I know you will return to being the same Max Porter I fell in love with when love and marriage were the furthest things from my mind. I have never regretted our life together, not for one moment. What I am about to tell you is very important to me, and I want you to promise to understand and consider it seriously.

In all the years of our marriage you never said or did anything that made me unhappy. On the contrary, you did everything you could to make me happy. It was a mission you undertook, and you succeeded admirably. I always considered it your gift to me. But now I realize that it was more than that. You were happy making me happy, so we were both happy together! Our happiness together was the gift.

After I'm gone, it might be that you will meet a woman who has qualities you admire, perhaps the same qualities you loved in me. If the possibility arises, please don't turn your back on it in deference to my memory. You see, darling, if you make another woman as happy as you have made me, it will be as though I were still with you. I know she would be someone as special as you always said I was and you would be happy together. That's what I want for you. It would pain me terribly if you were lonely because you thought you shouldn't be happy with someone else.

The letter ended abruptly, for more had been beyond Dorothy's strength. Max folded the letter and put it away in his pocket. He bent over Dorothy's frail form and kissed her. She opened her eyes and smiled, and Max knew she was waiting for an answer. He placed his lips to her ear and whispered, "I promise."

Max had never considered the possibility of finding someone else. He was content with his memories of Dorothy. They had fulfilled him. Opportunities had presented themselves. A widower with Max's qualities and resources was a sought-after prize. Max had had no interest. But now he had met Marion, and he remembered his promise.

chapter 10

WHEN MAX RETURNED FROM HIS reverie, he was in Summit
City. He headed for a group of shops not far from his old
neighborhood. Parking his car as close as he could, he walked toward a
store sandwiched between a Superette and a Laundromat. A neon sign
in the shape of a motion picture projector with rotating reels of film
hung in its window and flashed *CINEMABILIA* in blazing red, blue, and
green. Max entered and looked around.

"It hasn't changed. I don't suppose it ever will," he reflected.

There were cases and shelves loaded with videos and DVDs, tables
holding cartons of eight-by-ten glossy photos along with racks of movie
posters and lobby cards. The back wall was lined with shelves that held
collectables and books relating to the movies. Behind the wall in a large
back room was a film library of sixteen and super-eight-millimeter
classic silent and early sound films.

"Dave!" Max called. "Where the hell are you?"

"Keep your shirt on. I'm coming," a voice roared from the back room.

Dave Benjamin was a big man. He came from the back room,
shuffling his six-foot-two, 220-pound frame through the doorway. He
wore corduroy trousers and a plaid flannel shirt with a red bandana
tied cowboy-style around his neck. On his feet a pair of large terry-cloth

carpet slippers accounted for his shuffling gait. If his size was imposing, his face was impressive! His features might have been chiseled by an ancient Greek sculptor and left to weather until the hard edges had softened and only the strength remained. It was an actor's face. Those familiar with Dave's past knew he had been an actor. Those who knew nothing of his past felt he should have been.

"Max Porter! I thought I recognized that mellifluous voice. So you decided to come back to civilization?"

"Just a visit," replied Max, "and to do some business with you. By the way, Dave, how is business?"

"Retail is off, but I attribute that to your moving away. You were my best customer. How I loved taking your money away from you, but all good things, as they say. Now mail order and the Internet! That's a different story. I can't keep up with all the orders. And to think I almost didn't listen to you when you laid it all out for me! I owe you for that one, Max."

"Think nothing of it, Dave. I had to do something to keep you around. If you folded, who would take my money? After all, what are friends for?"

"So, friend, how come you haven't come back to see me before this?" Dave demanded.

"I wanted to, but I had some trouble adjusting to my new surroundings. I was afraid if I got involved with all the old things I was used to, especially the films, I'd blow the whole Amberfields thing, and that would have upset my son. I had to give it time."

"And it's okay now?"

"Yes, Dave, it's okay. Amberfields is a completely different place for me now."

"Good! Now maybe I can start taking your money away from you again."

"As a matter of fact, you can. I need copies of *Nanook of the North* and *Waikiki Wedding.*

"Film?" Dave asked.

"No, VHS or DVD."

Dave thought for a moment. "You're in luck. I have copies of both in VHS." He left and returned in a few moments and handed Max two video cassettes. "Not the most popular titles in my stock."

"They are to me," replied Max.

Dave suspected there was a woman behind this transformation, but he respected Max's privacy too much to make mention of it. "I have something else to go with *Waikiki Wedding*," he said. He picked up a large carton sitting on the floor near the front door and placed it on the table that held the glossy photos.

"A guy walked in here a few days ago with this carton and offered to sell it to me. It contains over a hundred copies of sheet music from the twenties and thirties, mostly songs featured in motion pictures. I asked him how much he wanted for it and he said, 'Twenty-five bucks.' Max, fifty would have been cheap. I gave him the twenty-five, and now I feel guilty about it. Some of these sheets could go for over a hundred dollars."

As he talked, Dave was rummaging through the contents of the carton. Finally he found what he was looking for, removed it, and handed it to Max. The coarsely screened blue, red, and orange images jumped off the glossy surface of its cover, revealing the original sheet music for the song "Sweet Leilani".

Before he said anything, Max opened the sheet and read the lyrics. One verse caught his eye as being particularly relevant. "This is perfect, Dave."

"Consider it my gift to you and your Sweet Leilani. If you like, I'll have it framed for you."

"Thanks, Dave, but I think I prefer it this way."

Dave studied Max. "You've got it pretty bad, old buddy, haven't you?"

"I'm not sure, Dave. All I know is that I like being with her. She's the first woman I've been comfortable with since Dorothy passed away. When you meet her, you'll understand."

"And when will that be?"

"Soon, Dave, very soon, I hope."

chapter 11

THE PACKAGE CAME BY OVERNIGHT express. Marion was curious. She hadn't ordered anything, and the sender, Cinemabilia, was unknown to her. She tore open the package, and when she saw the contents, she knew even without reading the attached letter who the sender was. She took out the two videos and read the titles and then opened the letter.

Dear Mrs. Wade (AKA Leilani),

We had such a pleasant introduction that I felt it would not be misconstrued if I offered these videos of the films that came up in our conversation. I must apologize for the haste of my action, but film collectors are uncontrolled evangelists, crusaders for the glory of the Golden Age of Film. Enjoy.

With kindest personal regards,

Sincerely,

Max Porter (AKA Nanook)

PS. Would you know anyone who might be interested in a pair of slightly used mukluks?

Marion sighed, and then she smiled. His seeking out copies of these rather obscure titles for her was such a lovely gesture. She put the videos down on the table and reread the letter. The simple directness of the note, the humor, even the apology for rushing to send them impressed her. There was no overture, no hidden meaning, not even a mention of a future meeting. Max Porter was an old-school gentleman, she thought, and he was very attractive. Yes, she reflected, very attractive. She saw him with her mind's eye as she had seen him in the mail room, his craggy features set in a slightly lined, handsome face crowned by a crop of gray hair mixed with just enough black to give it the sheen of brushed pewter. She savored the vision. Edna Canfield was right. Max Porter was someone worth knowing.

But then she heard the voice. *Five minutes, Marion, you've only talked to him for five minutes. You can't really learn anything in five minutes.*

"But he's a gentleman. I know that much," she told the voice. "You read the letter. Could he be anything else?"

So he's a gentleman. He's attractive and he wears his clothes well. And he writes a great letter. But so did Carl. Marion, have you forgotten Carl and what that gentleman did to you?

Marion had been holding the letter. She glanced at it and put it down next to the videos. "No, I haven't forgotten ... *or what I did to him.* I'll never forget."

Then go easy. Don't let him charm you. Keep him at a distance. Time will tell who he really is.

"I have to thank him for these videos." Marion reached for the telephone, held it for a moment, and then replaced the receiver without dialing. "I can't just phone to thank him and let it go at that. It wouldn't be fair. No, I'll have to thank him in person. And anyway, I don't think he would want me to call and ask to see him. He would want the privilege of asking me. No, the telephone is out, but a chance meeting, perhaps in the dining room—" Marion looked at her watch. It was lunchtime. She grabbed her handbag and started for the door.

Be careful, Marion. But Marion was no longer listening.

chapter 12

MAX WAITED ALL MORNING, HOPING that Marion would call. It was almost noon, and as the minutes dragged by, a pall of disappointment hung over him. He wondered if she had received the videos. He had paid extra for morning delivery. *Should I call her?* he thought. *No, that wouldn't be right. She might think I was rushing her.* He gave in to his frustration. *I'm too old for this sort of thing,* he thought. *This is a young man's game!*

Max decided to go into the city and have lunch, and it was about time to see the old gang. He could face them now. He got a jacket and the keys to his Buick and headed out. When he reached the door to the parking garage, he changed his mind. There was a perfectly good dining room here in the building, and he hoped Marion might be there. He'd settle for another chance meeting. He turned and headed back the way he'd come. Then he went into the corridor that led to the dining room. On his left were windows that looked out on the lower lake, and he paused to take in the view. The water glistened as a breeze created a kaleidoscope of ripples that danced in the reflected sunlight. It was his kind of day, a day to be out in the sun and fresh air. For a moment he wavered. He really didn't feel like eating, and a walk around the lake with the chance of skipping a few stones might cure this funk he felt building up. Then he thought of Marion. Not hearing from her, not seeing her, that was the cause of his funk. He had to work this out. He turned away from the window and headed for the dining room.

Sitting at their usual table, Edna and Arthur Canfield were just finishing their lunch when Arthur, who was in the process of informing Edna that he intended to have dessert regardless of her objections, stopped in midsentence as Edna raised her hand and waved toward the entrance. He turned in the direction of her waving hand and saw Marion Wade respond and approach them.

"Sit down and join us," Edna said when Marion reached their table.

"Thanks," replied Marion. "I really don't feel like eating alone."

"Problem?" Edna asked.

Thinking quickly, Marion responded, "Oh no, it's just that I had plans for today that didn't work out. You know how that is."

"We certainly do. Don't we, Arthur?"

"Yes, we do!" responded Arthur, his dessert coming to mind.

The ever-attentive Sid came to the table with menu in hand. "Good afternoon, Mrs. Wade."

"Hello, Sid. I'll just have a turkey club and coffee."

As Sid turned to deliver Marion's order to the kitchen, Arthur called out, "Just a minute, Sid. I'd like a crème brûlée."

"I'm sorry, Mr. Canfield. Brûlée is only served at dinner. Perhaps a sherry custard?"

Edna spoke up, "Make it a small piece of angel food cake, Sid. But no whipped cream! Not even on the side." As Sid left, she looked at Arthur, "You slipped that in very nicely, dear, but remember, there will be no dessert for you tonight!"

"Thank you, my sweet," he said, blowing her a kiss. Edna responded by wrinkling her nose and squinting her eyes, forming an almost rabbit-like face. She tilted her head, puckered her lips, and snapped a kiss back to Arthur. Then she reached out and placed her hand on his. The tableau ended as the two octogenarians sprang back to reality and cackled like teenagers.

"You see how it is, Marion? This grown man has an insatiable sweet tooth. If I didn't monitor his diet, he'd be a three-hundred-pound diabetic instead of a 170-pound hunk." She turned back to Arthur. "And then who would love you?"

"I won't let that happen, Edna, my love. I like being your hunk."

Marion sat listening, fascinated by the exchange. Here were two people still very much in love, and they didn't care who knew it. *How wonderful*, she thought. How wonderful it would have been if Carl had been more like Arthur and she more like Edna. In the latter years of their marriage there had been nothing more than formal dialogue, not any of the humor and contentment with each other that was exhibited by Edna and Arthur. Worst of all, there could be no outward sign of love. She wondered how she'd survived as long as she had.

Sid arrived with Marion's turkey club and Arthur's angel food cake. All attention was fixed on Sid as he laid a place setting in front of Marion before he put the sandwich down and poured her coffee. Then he moved on to Arthur as his cake was placed before him. No one noticed Max Porter approaching the table.

Max had seen them as soon as he had entered the dining room. Marion was there with the Canfields. He was relieved to see her but had hoped to be alone with her. He was uncertain whether to go directly to their table or wait until one of them saw him and waved him over. The waiter was fussing over the table, and Max was worried that they might not see him. "Oh, hell, nothing ventured, nothing gained," Max told himself as he made his way to their table.

Arthur surveyed the cake with mixed emotions. It was dessert, but in size and sweetness it was but a dry morsel. He looked up and scanned the table for sympathy. It was then that he saw Max approaching.

"Hello, Max. Sit down and help me with this piece of cake," he said with a touch of sarcastic humor. "I'll never be able to finish it by myself!"

"Thanks, Arthur, but I'd like to have some lunch first. Save me a piece."

Edna spoke up, "Sid, would you bring a chair for Mr. Porter?" As Sid turned to pull a chair from another table, Edna noticed the look that passed between Max and Marion. Max hadn't taken his eyes from Marion. She acknowledged his gaze and then demurely lowered her eyes and toyed with the toothpick holding her sandwich together.

"You've met Marion Wade, haven't you, Max?"

Without looking away from Marion, Max replied, "Yes, we met yesterday in the mail room. How are you today, Mrs. Wade?"

"Just fine, Mr. Porter. And you?"

"Very fine, Mrs. Wade. Thank you."

Sid had placed the chair opposite Marion so that when Max sat down, they were facing each other.

"Can I take your order, Mr. Porter?"

"Mrs. Wade's club sandwich looks good. I'll have the same, but with the mayo on the side ... and coffee."

"Watching your fat intake, Max?" asked Edna. "I wish I could get Arthur to watch his."

"Actually it's more for neatness than health reasons. Club sandwiches can get pretty messy if too much mayonnaise is slathered on. You bite down and all the contents slither out and at best, wind up on your plate or worse, in your lap. I prefer to spread a little mayo on the edge of each quarter of the club. That way I get the taste of the mayo, and the sandwich holds together."

When he finished, he realized his long-winded explanation made him sound like a pompous ass. Color rose and tinted his face. He wondered what Marion was thinking of him now.

"That's ingenious," exclaimed Arthur. "It's like having your club sandwich and eating it too!"

"Pay no attention to Arthur, Max," Edna said. "He's jealous because he's not allowed to have mayonnaise. His cholesterol, you know." She turned to Arthur. "Isn't that so, Arthur?"

"But I can have angel food cake. Can't I, my love?"

Marion addressed Max, "One wonders, Mr. Porter, if the demise of your club sandwich lies less with the slathering and slithering than with the size of the bite."

She said it with the same lilt in her voice she had used in the mail room, and Max was once again enthralled. He knew that she was having fun with him, and he enjoyed it. Now it was his turn.

"Why, I do believe you're right, Mrs. Wade. Now that I think about it, a club sandwich is more a ladies' sandwich to be daintily held and eaten with small bites. You might say a sandwich to be nibbled. But a manly grasp and large bite will upset the delicate balance of the club sandwich's construction with calamitous results. Now I feel compelled to erase slathering and slithering from my vocabulary."

"There's no need for that, Mr. Porter. You never know when you might need slather and slither in the future. It pays to be prepared just in case."

"I can't foresee the need for their use again. They're not pretty words."

"But they are very descriptive words. If you ever had to describe the manly art of shaving, for example, what better verbal picture could you paint than the slather of the lather onto your face and the slither of the razor across your beard?"

Max looked across the table, and with bowed head, he said apologetically, "I'm sorry, but I could never use those two words to describe the art of shaving."

"Oh? Why is that?" questioned Marion.

"Because I use an electric razor," Max replied.

There was a moment of silence as they looked at one another. Then simultaneously they burst into laughter. When she could finally speak, Marion said, "Mr. Porter, I believe we have elevated nonsense to its highest plane."

"A noble endeavor, I would say," he replied.

The Canfields watched as this exchange unfolded. Arthur had some difficulty following the gist of the repartee but thought it very amusing and laughed when he thought it appropriate. Edna, on the other hand, read much more into the banter of these two supposed strangers. Marion and Max acted as though they had known each other forever. They seemed so at ease in each other's company that it was impossible to conceive of their having met less than twenty-four hours before. Edna wondered if they knew what they had found. Then she remembered the look that had passed between them and realized that they did know that they had found something wonderful. All they needed was time for it to blossom. They were a love affair waiting to happen. She resolved to help them along.

"Arthur, have you forgotten your promise to me?"

"I probably have, my love. What did I promise?"

"You promised to come to the mall with me so we can buy you some new slacks and a replacement for that ratty sport jacket you're wearing."

"Must we go now, my love? I haven't finished my cake."

"There is no time like the present. I'm sure that Marion and Max will excuse us."

chapter 13

AFTER THE CANFIELDS LEFT THE table, Marion, wanting to maintain the light mood that they seemed to fall into so easily, asked, "Was it something we said?"

Max chuckled. "Hardly. I think Edna wanted us to be alone together. She's a born matchmaker. I felt that when I first met her. She had that look in her eye. Her mental computer was searching a database for an eligible match. Now she thinks she's found it."

"I'm sure she means well. Don't let it upset you."

"It doesn't upset me. It's just that when two people meet as we have, it's up to them to find their own level of friendship. Outside influences, no matter how well intentioned, can create problems."

Sid came with Max's sandwich. He cleared away the Canfield's dishes and set a place for Max. When Sid finished and left, Max looked across the table. Marion was looking at him.

"Would you mind?" he said, indicating the seat to her left.

"Please do, Max."

He slid his plate and coffee cup over and then changed seats. "Much better," he said.

Marion watched him transfer to the closer seat. She realized that she was beginning to feel emotions that she hadn't allowed herself to feel for a long time. She liked watching Max, and she enjoyed being with him. She thought how nice it would be to reach over and put her hand on his as she had seen Edna do with Arthur, but it was only a thought. Then that inner voice of hers spoke and broke the spell. *He's serious, Marion. Keep it light. Don't become serious.* She obeyed the voice. "Well done, Max. You didn't spill a drop." It was about as light as she could get.

"I'm only clumsy when I'm completely vertical and never when there is food in front of me," Max replied. "Now while you nibble away at your sandwich, I shall attack mine without too much slathering or slithering." He reached for the dish of mayonnaise and started to paint the edge of his sandwich. He brought it to his mouth, and with a *manly* bite, he sent half the contents slithering onto his plate. Max looked at Marion. She shook her head as though to say, "Oh, Max," and handed him his knife and fork. "Maybe it isn't the mayonnaise," he said sheepishly and took the utensils. Marion had all she could do not to reach across and take the poor boy's hand. Before the voice had a chance to remind her to be careful, she laughed. Then Max laughed, and they laughed together at another shared moment.

Marion turned serious. "Max, I haven't had a chance to thank you for the videos. It was a wonderful gesture, and I appreciate it very much. I can't wait to see them. I just have to get something to play them on."

Max was amazed. It was hard to believe there were still people who didn't have VCR and DVD players. "No need to buy one," he said. "I have some in storage with my film equipment. I'll drive over tomorrow and pick one out and install it for you."

"But Max, you shouldn't," she protested. "I really—"

Before she could finish, Max interrupted, "Marion, don't you hate to see something good and useful packed away in a dark closet, forgotten and unused. Even a machine has a soul that cries out to be taken from the darkness into the light. So you see, you'll be rescuing it, giving back its life! And anyway, the videos have no value unless you can see them."

Marion wondered if he was talking about machines or himself. She felt it necessary to keep it light.

"Max Porter, you are incorrigible!"

"So you've noticed? It's one of my many wholesome attributes. I hope to display all of them to you in time. By the way, have you noticed that as soon as the Canfields left, we began calling each other by our first names?"

"It seemed the natural thing to do. Actually I was going to call you Nanook, but I didn't think you felt like that old Eskimo any longer. You don't, do you, Max?"

Max thought for a moment before he replied, "Not in the least. It's amazing how rejuvenating a new friend can be, and Marion, I felt that we were going to be friends as soon as we met in the mail room. We are friends, aren't we?"

"Yes, Max, we're friends, and we've probably broken the world's record for two people meeting and becoming friends. We've known each other a little over twenty-four hours, but we've only been face-to-face for about half an hour. That has to be a record of some kind."

Max laughed and said, "Sort of *friends at first sight.*"

Marion thought that over and then responded, "Friends at first sight." But she couldn't help wondering about the implications.

They sat there for another hour, alternately nibbling at their sandwiches and talking, mostly talking. They were enjoying each other's company, the dining room and the food just a stage and props for the play that was unfolding. Max ordered a lightly mixed fresh fruit dessert and coffee. Marion just had coffee. When it came, Max slid the fruit bowl between them and handed Marion a fork. She should refuse, she thought, but in fact, she liked the idea. She took the fork, and together they grazed from the bowl. It was their first intimate moment, and both thought it a perfectly natural thing to do. Their relationship was now firmly established by a bowl of fruit salad.

chapter 14

THE FOLLOWING MORNING MAX WAITED until 9:30 before he called Marion. He had given the call a lot of thought. He knew what he wanted to say to her, but even after he had mulled it over in his head since he had awakened at five, he couldn't put the words together. Now he was standing with the receiver pressed to his ear, counting the rings. By the third ring he began losing his nerve and considered hanging up. But the fourth ring had barely started when it was replaced by an hello.

"Good morning, Marion. I hope I didn't wake you."

Marion recognized his voice immediately. "No, Max. I've been up for ages."

"I'm glad," he said and realized that it hadn't come out right. "I mean I'm glad about not waking you, not about your being up for ages." He was ten years old again.

"Yes, Max, I knew what you meant."

"Well, I was wondering." He was faltering, and after a pause he continued, "Are you doing anything today?"

"Why do you ask?"

Good! She left the door open, he thought to himself. He was an adult again. "I'm driving into the city to pick up the tape player. I thought you might like to come along. You could see the collection." He was speaking faster than usual. He didn't want to give her an opportunity to refuse until he had laid out his whole plan for the day. He raced on, "And afterward we could stop for lunch. There's a very nice restaurant not far from the storage company, small but popular. The food is excellent, and the setting is very relaxing. Say yes, and I'll call for a reservation."

Marion was thrilled at the invitation, but her inner voice screamed, *Too soon, Marion! Too soon! Be careful!*

"I'd like to go, Max, but I don't know if—" Her voice trailed off.

Max didn't understand Marion's reluctance. He couldn't see beyond the sincerity of his offer. "Is anything wrong?" he asked.

Marion hesitated. How could she tell him he was coming on too strong? She needed time to examine her feelings. The feelings were coming from her heart. That much she knew. But was that enough? So had it been with Carl, at least in the beginning. She mustn't make that mistake again.

But she was smarter now. She could handle it. She would never know the real Max Porter by pushing him away or the real Marion Wade either.

"No, Max, nothing is wrong. I had planned to do some shopping, but I can do that tomorrow. What time do you want to leave?"

"Would right now be too soon?"

Keep it light, she thought. "Max, did you forget I'm a woman? I need at least a half an hour to get ready. Now you'll get the opportunity to show me another of your many wholesome attributes."

"Which one is that?" he asked.

"Patience, Max. It's probably the most important attribute when dealing with a woman. I'll be ready in thirty minutes."

Max came down ten minutes early. He checked the armchairs scattered around the lobby, chose one that offered a front-on view of the elevators, and sat down. Exactly twenty-three minutes from the time she had hung up the phone, Marion floated out of the elevator and came toward him. Max sprang from his chair and hurried to meet her. They stood with only their eyes touching until Marion broke the spell.

"Did I keep you waiting?"

"Actually you're seven minutes early. We'll put those seven minutes into your time bank. If in future you're ever late, we'll draw on the seven minutes and cancel out your tardiness. That way you'll always be on time."

Marion laughed. "My math isn't good enough to understand how you arrived at that piece of wizardry, but I'll accept it with thanks. I do hate to be tardy."

They turned and headed out of the lobby. Max's car was waiting. As the parking attendant held the door open for Marion, Max stepped forward and placed his hand on Marion's elbow to assist her. Making no comment, she stiffened and pulled her arm away. Max attributed it to a sudden loss of balance and thought no more of it. He backed away, and the attendant closed the door. Max tipped him and walked around to the driver's side.

The drive to town usually took forty-five to fifty minutes, but if you were in a hurry to get somewhere and if traffic cooperated, then you could make it in about thirty minutes. But Max had no intention of hurrying. He was behind the wheel of his Buick, something he always enjoyed, and sitting beside him was someone he enjoyed being with. They casually chatted as the miles rolled away, and before they knew it, they were on the outskirts of Summit City. Ten minutes later they pulled into the storage company's parking lot. After they registered and went through the security routine, Max drove to a bank of garage-like structures and parked in front of one of them. He got out, walked around the car, opened the passenger door, and offered his hand to assist Marion. After a moment's hesitation she took his hand and exited the car. He was too pleased with her company to notice her hesitation.

Max punched his security code into a keypad. The overhead door rose, and the lights went on to expose a space about the size of a large two-car garage. Almost half the space was filled with odd shapes draped with sheets, which Marion assumed to be furniture. Along one wall were metal shelves with stacks of neatly labeled cans of film. In front of the shelves were cartons arranged to form aisles, each carton labeled with a large red number.

"It doesn't look like much, stuffed away here, but it's everything of importance I couldn't take with me to Amberfields."

Marion knew how he felt. She had also given up many of her

possessions in order to relocate to Amberfields. A response was unnecessary. Max understood.

They crossed the threshold, and Max turned to a table just inside the door. He picked up a clipboard from the table and flipped through the attached papers until he found the one he wanted and scanned it with his finger. "Carton eight, item three," he said aloud but to himself. He put the clipboard back on the table, picked up a utility knife and a tape dispenser, and started for carton eight. He hadn't noticed that Marion had wandered off and was standing by the racks that held the film cans, reading their labels.

She turned to Max. "This is amazing, Max. The actual films just like they show in the theater. I know about collecting tapes and DVDs, but I didn't know the films were available for collecting."

"They're not really the actual films, Marion," Max explained. "These are copies of the original films reproduced for various reasons in a smaller size. The content is the same."

During Max's explanation Marion continued along the racks, studying the titles. Suddenly she stopped and exclaimed, "Max, these are Lone Star movies! You have Lone Star movies!"

"All the titles that are available. Some are lost, but every once in a while a lost one will turn up in a barn in Poland or in someone's attic. Someday I hope to have the complete library of Lone Star films. I keep working on it. I have a special interest in Lone Star."

Marion smiled. Here was another common interest. "So have I," she said. "He was my first true love! I was ten years old when I saw my first Lone Star movie. It was *They Call Me Lone Star.* I was a terrible tomboy then, and all I wanted was to be a cowgirl and ride off into the sunset alongside Lone Star. I'd love to see them again."

"And so you shall. I'll consider it a command performance. I'll even invite Lone Star himself to attend."

Marion's eyes almost popped. "You mean the real Lone Star? You know Lone Star?" She was as excited as a young child learning there was a Santa Claus.

"Yes, Marion, there is a real Lone Star. He's alive and kicking, and he lives right here in Summit City. His real name is Dave Benjamin, and he's one of my dearest friends."

"Please can we see him today?"

"My goodness, you're impatient. I think I'm going to be jealous. He may not be available today, but I'll set it up as soon as possible. Now let's get what we came for."

"I can't believe it. I'm actually going to meet Lone Star," she said as they headed to carton eight.

At carton eight Max knelt and slit the tape and opened the carton. "Item three," he repeated as he removed bubble-wrapped packages marked with large black numbers and laid them on the floor. Item three finally appeared. He removed it and set it down beside Marion and then replaced the other items and resealed the carton.

They returned to the table, and Max removed the bubble wrap. He enumerated the contents for Marion's benefit. "One combination DVD/VCR player, one set of connecting cables, one remote—batteries not included, I have plenty—one instruction manual, which isn't necessary. You have me and my technical service that is available 24-7 365 days a year."

"That sounds as though you come with carton eight, item three." As soon as she said it, she realized that what she had intended to be a lighthearted reply could be misconstrued.

Before she could say anything more, Max replied, "In spirit only. However, I do offer a no-strings-attached guarantee. You just have to call to take advantage of my service. And there will never be a charge *of any kind!*"

Marion felt the first rumblings of the voice. She was not going to let the voice spoil this day. *Blot it out*, she told herself. *I can't hear it if I keep talking.* "A no-strings guarantee and no charge ... ever," she exclaimed. "That's what I call customer service!"

Max smiled and bowed. "At your service, ma'am."

"Now where is that lunch you promised me?"

Evidently the voice was also hungry. It didn't utter another word.

chapter 15

"IT'S CHARMING," MARION REMARKED AS they waited to be seated.

Momma Maria's was small. Marion counted twelve tables, eight of which were occupied. A short, motherly woman whom Marion supposed to be Momma Maria hurried to welcome them. "Mr. Porter, it is good to see you again. It has been too long. And now you bring with you this beautiful lady." She smiled and extended her hand to Marion.

Max remembered his manners. "Momma, may I present Marion Wade, a friend and neighbor."

"You are most welcome, Marion Wade. I am happy that Mr. Porter has brought you to my restaurant."

Marion felt the welcome in Momma's plump hand and in the glow of her smile. The intimacy of the little restaurant warmed her. She was blushing and felt embarrassed to display such a schoolgirl reaction.

"I'm so happy to meet you, Momma Maria. Mr. Porter only told me that he knew of a little restaurant that served wonderful food. It's the first time since we met that he understated anything. Your restaurant is charming."

Momma feigned a pout. "Not even *one* superlative from Mr. Porter? I am disappointed. I had better make this lunch one to be remembered."

Momma Maria led them to a corner table, and when they were seated, she turned and headed to the kitchen. "She'll be right back," Max remarked. "She went to get our lunch started."

"But we haven't ordered yet," Marion exclaimed.

Max smiled. "There's no menu. When you come to Momma's, you are treated as a guest in her home. You will find her lunch to be light, varied, and satisfying. You won't be disappointed. I guarantee it."

Marion laughed. "Another guarantee? You do take customer service seriously."

"But this one has strings attached. You'll want to come back, but I'm going to tell Momma not to let you in unless you are accompanied by me."

"You would do that?"

"Of course. I have an interest to protect."

"And this interest, is it honorable?"

"May I be drawn and quartered if it is anything but."

Marion wanted to reach out and take his hand, but she was afraid of the voice. The only voice she wanted to hear was Max's. The voice would have to wait until tonight when she was alone.

"Drawn and quartered! I doubt it will ever come to that."

Momma was standing beside the kitchen door, waiting. She couldn't hear any of their conversation, but she sensed that Mr. Porter and his lady were sharing an important moment. It was best not to interrupt. When there was a lull in their conversation and the couple sat smiling into each other's eyes, Momma seized the moment and approached their table. She carried a tray with an opened bottle of wine and two glasses. She placed the glasses on the table and filled them.

"A special occasion should always start with a special wine," she said. "Now toast each other while I get your antipasto."

As soon as the kitchen door closed behind Momma's ample figure, what started as spontaneous smiles built to full-blown laughter that they quickly stifled.

"Dear Momma," said Marion, "she'll have us engaged by the antipasto and the wedding date set before dessert. She's wonderful."

"She's already working out the wedding reception menu," Max added. Although he thought it was a wonderful idea, he didn't pursue it.

They fell silent. Max was savoring the moment. Marion mentally clamped her hands over her ears to block out the voice that had started chanting, *Too soon! Too soon!*

Max lifted his glass and looked into Marion's eyes, "To Sweet Leilani, AKA Marion Wade, friend at first sight."

Marion lifted her glass in turn, "To Nanook, late of the North, AKA Max Porter, a dear friend at first sight."

They touched glasses and sealed the toast. Marion put her glass down. "It's becoming more than that, isn't it, Max?"

"More then friends at first sight?" he asked.

"You know what I mean. I'm not sure that I'm ready to become that deeply involved. I know how I feel when I'm with you, but—"

He took her hand in his, raised it to his lips, and gently kissed her fingers. She didn't flinch at his touch as she had done before. "You must know how I feel about you," he said. "I haven't done a very good job of hiding it."

"This thing we feel, Max, is it real or just something of the moment? We could end up hating each other."

Max gently squeezed her hand. "Do you really think that could happen to us?"

Marion withdrew her hand. She looked pensive as though she was thinking back to another time. "It could," she said.

"You sound as though it has happened before."

Marion didn't respond. She was afraid Max would press for details, and this was neither the time nor the place. "Max, this morning I told you that patience is necessary when dealing with a woman. Now I'm asking you to be patient. I need time to—" She hesitated, afraid to tell Max about the voice or what had happened on the night her husband died. "To get used to the idea of being with a man again and making a commitment I'll never want to break."

Max took back her hand. It was cold, but he felt the warmth return as he held it in his. "Of course I'll be patient. But if it will help any, Marion, I'm fully committed to spending the rest of my life trying to make you happy. I'm available now if you need help getting rid of bad memories. It's part of my customer service, and I guarantee it. Now let's forget about the demons of the past and enjoy Momma Maria's lunch."

They were still holding hands when Momma came with the antipasto.

It was late afternoon when they started back to Amberfields. At first they spoke little, preferring to quietly savor the memory of their day together. It wasn't until they were out of the city and on County Route 217 that Marion spoke. "You were so right about Momma's. It was a wonderful lunch, and Momma was so—" Marion hesitated, searching for the proper word.

"Perceptive?" offered Max.

"We weren't too obvious, were we?"

"No more than the average neon sign. Momma could hardly miss it."

Marion was silent again for a few moments, and then haltingly she asked, "Did you mind, Max? We were acting like a couple of teenagers."

"A couple of teenagers on their first date, and I sincerely hope it's the first of many to come. How could I mind? I haven't felt this good in ages. It's like starting to live again. I feel like I'm floating on a cloud." He took his eyes from the road and glanced at Marion, "I hope you feel the same way because the only thing that could bring me down from that cloud is if you didn't have as good a time as I had."

"It was lovely," she replied. "I can't recall ever having a day like this. It was a new experience, something that never happened in my twenty-three years of marriage."

Max was surprised. It needed explaining. "How so?" he asked.

"It seemed that everything you did or said today was to make me happy. I've never encountered anything like that before, and I'm not certain how to react."

Max laughed and said, "You're doing just fine, and the day's not over yet. When we get back, I'll install the video player, and we can watch the movies. By the way, you do have a television set that I can hook the player into?"

Marion was glad of the change of subject. Now it was her turn to laugh. "And what would you do if I didn't have a television set?"

"Not a problem. I'd bring over my little portable. Unfortunately it has a small screen and we'd have to sit very close together to see the picture."

"Sorry to disappoint you, but I have a beautiful large flat-screen TV with lots of bells and whistles. I'm sure you'll have great fun playing with it."

"So you have a really big TV! I hope you left enough room for a kitchenette?"

Marion wondered what Max was leading up to. "Of course I have a kitchenette and a dining area too."

"Good. After I hook up the player, I'll rustle up a couple of my famous omelets. I have all the fixings in my refrigerator. I'll bring them with the tools."

"Why bother? We could go down to the dining room."

"Actually I want to show off another of my wholesome attributes. Every little bit helps. And to be perfectly honest, I don't want to share you tonight with a restaurant full of senior citizens."

chapter 16

IT WAS PAST FIVE WHEN Max and Marion returned to Amberfields. "I'll just stop at my apartment and pick up my tools and the fixings for the omelets," Max said as they waited for the elevator. "That is, of course, if it's okay. I don't want to impose or overstay my welcome."

"Of course it's all right, Max. The shopping I had planned for today was food shopping. My cupboard is bare. By the way, I've also been known to whip up a pretty good omelet myself. I can make the omelets while you're doing whatever you do with the TV. We can watch the movies while we eat."

"That's fine with me, except—"

"Except?" she questioned.

"Dinner is for conversation. We'll have plenty of time for the movies after dinner."

Max realized that he might have offended Marion by appearing bossy. He hastened to soften his statement with humor.

"I think I read that somewhere, or maybe I just made it up. Can we discuss it over dinner?"

"I think we'll have other things to discuss over dinner."

"Now that's encouraging!"

"Is that a leer forming on your face? Just don't get too encouraged.

Remember, patience is one of your wholesome attributes, or so you said. And we have two films to watch after dinner. Now I have to freshen up, so you had best scurry off to your apartment and do the same."

Back in her apartment Marion did a quick washup, ran a comb through her hair, and changed into a pair of jeans and a bulky wool pullover. As she inspected herself in her full-length mirror, the voice broke its silence.

What's the matter with you? Don't you know he's the enemy? And you've invited him in ... letting the enemy in! You know what he'll do. He'll do what all men do when they want something. He'll do what Carl did!

Marion turned from the mirror and cried out, "No! He's not like that! He's thoughtful and kind and funny and very gentle, things I've never known in any man before ... and I love him!"

Love him? You are a silly girl! For twenty-three years you loved Carl, and how did he return your love? Do I have to spell it out for you? Men don't give love. They only take love. Max Porter is no different. He will force upon you what he wants. If not tonight, then soon! Mark me, Marion, before it's too late!

The ringing telephone drowned out the voice. Marion sensed who was calling and quickly regained her composure. She picked up the phone and heard Max's voice, "Have you freshened up? Is it okay to come over?"

"Where is that patience that is supposed to be one of your wholesome attributes?" she teased. Then with that sweet lilt in her voice that Max loved so much, she said, "You'll have to hold out for another five minutes."

"I'll walk slowly," he replied.

"Very slowly!" she responded.

Five minutes later Max appeared at her door, carrying two shopping bags filled with eggs, bread, cheese, ham, various vegetables, and two bottles of wine (one for dinner and one for the films). His jacket pockets bulged with an assortment of small tools.

"Porter's Culinary and TV Service," he said as he maneuvered the two overstuffed shopping bags through the doorway. "Point me toward the kitchen, milady, and I shall distribute these comestibles to a better place than whence they came. Then to the TV dragon that I shall subdue and charge to obey the commands of the new magical remote, Merlin."

Marion laughed. Here was her champion, the prince of Amberfields.

She didn't know what tonight would bring, but she trusted Max ... and herself. For a moment Marion feared the voice would speak and spoil everything. But never fear, she told herself, her champion would ride to the rescue and slay the demon. Marion smiled. She thought she could hear the voice gasping for breath.

"Such largesse, milord. I am overwhelmed by your generosity."

"It is a mere token of my affection, milady. Were it but diamonds."

"But it is written, one cannot make an omelet with diamonds."

"It is also written that if one eats alone, it is merely the intake of sustenance, but when two dine together, it is a feast. Hence, the magnitude of my offering."

"But seriously all this food for one meal is too much for two people."

"I suppose so, but when you said your cupboard was bare, I took a look into mine, and as usual, I had much too much. I always overbuy. I guess it's because I hate food shopping. I stock up so I won't have to shop so often, and I figured a little redistribution would be in order. After all, I did take you away from your shopping today."

"That's very sweet, Max, but now you'll have to go shopping to replace—"

Max broke in before she could finish. "Not for another week. I'm still well stocked. Now I'll help put the stuff away, and then I'll go and do battle with the TV."

"No, you go do your battle, and I'll take care of the home front. And don't bang your thumb with a hammer. I don't want you coming back wounded."

"Fear not, milady. I did not bring a hammer," he said as he turned and made for the TV.

As he worked, Max listened to the sounds coming from the kitchenette, his mind putting pictures to the sounds. In the theater of his mind he saw Marion in the kitchenette, chopping the vegetables, grating the cheese, beating the eggs. He heard the clank of the pan as it met the stove, the sizzle of the eggs as Marion poured them into the hot pan, humming as she worked. Max was overcome by the domesticity of the scene, and an emotion he hadn't felt since before Dorothy had become ill overcame him. He felt at home and grateful to this woman who was making it possible. He snapped back to reality as he heard Marion call from the kitchenette.

"Are you finished, Max? Dinner's almost ready."

"Almost done. Just another minute or two."

chapter 17

THE TABLE WAS SET IN a dining area alongside the kitchenette. It was small and just about right for two people to sit opposite each other. At first Max was concerned that he would have difficulty reaching across the crowded table to take Marion's hand. He would be embarrassed if he upset the bottle of wine.

Marion came to the table, carrying two steaming plates. "Hot stuff," she said as a warning to Max, who was pouring the wine.

Max looked up at Marion and said, "I'll say!"

"Now stop that!" she reproached Max with a smile. But she really enjoyed Max's humorous compliment.

Max raised his glass. "A toast," he said, "to you, Marion. You made this a premier day, a model for all the days to come."

"That was lovely, Max. But today was just as much your doing as mine."

"Okay, if it will make you feel better, I'll amend the toast. To two people who together create beautiful days."

"That's even lovelier, and I'll drink to that. Now eat your omelet before it gets cold."

As they ate, Max became pensive. He had something on his mind. At first Marion expected a proposal, and she was prepared to remind him of his promise of patience. But then she sensed that it was something else. It wasn't the omelet. He devoured it, even admitting that her omelet recipe was much better than his.

"Where is that conversation you recommended having with dinner?" she asked.

Max snapped back from his thoughts. "I'm so sorry, Marion. I did drift away there for a while. Forgive me?"

"There's nothing to forgive, Max. But you looked as though something were disturbing you. Is it us?"

He reached across the table and took her hand. "Of course not!" Then he paused, as one would at the end of a high diving board, seeking balance before plunging in. "I was just reflecting on today. It was—" He didn't like the sound of the past tense and quickly corrected it. "It is such a wonderful day. I guess I was dreaming of all the wonderful days and nights we could have together. But there is something that disturbs me about my dreams."

Marion was apprehensive. She remembered his comment about demons of the past, and she was afraid he was going to bring it up again. "Is it something you can share with me?"

"Marion, honey, I want to share everything with you. I haven't thought about much else since we met in the mail room. I dream about things we could do, places we could go, always together. The dreams are clear, the images sharp, but they always end while we are doing those things. I never see us at home or even going home to Amberfields. The dreams just fade to black, as they say in the movies. Marion, does it mean we aren't going to be married?" He looked down at her hand curled in his and gently squeezed. Then he slowly raised his eyes to meet hers. "It has to be marriage, you know. I couldn't have it any other way."

"Oh, darling, I'm so glad you said that. Of course we are going to be married ... and soon. Be patient for a little while longer. And now I'm the one to guarantee it."

He wanted to leap across the table and scoop her up in his arms, but from the look in her eyes he felt that she wanted to say something more. He hoped she was ready to tell him why she needed more time and what her demon was. If he knew, he might be able to help her exorcize it, and they could get on with their life together. Marion's voice brought him out of his reverie.

"I think I know why your daydreams always end the way they do. You're still not happy at Amberfields. You want us to be somewhere else. But you know I like Amberfields, and you don't want to take me away from here. That's part of it, isn't it, Max?"

"You know, honey, you're amazing! We've known each other for just the blink of an eye, and in that short time you know me better than I know myself. I couldn't help falling in love with you. You're right. I'm not happy at Amberfields. Before I met you, Amberfields was a place of exile, a place where I didn't fit in or ever could fit in. We met, and you saved me from drifting away on that ice floe I created for myself.

"After I met you, Amberfields became tolerable, but only because you were here. I fell in love with you, and I wanted to be near you. I needed to court you because it was the only way I knew of winning you."

"Well, you'll be happy to know you've succeeded admirably. I loved every minute of it. And after we're married, I hope you will continue to court me. We could take turns courting each other."

"That's a happy thought, and if I'm not mistaken, that's a leer forming on your face."

"Oh, you're an elephant. You never forget anything. But seriously, darling, I think it's more than Amberfields. It's an age thing, isn't it? To you, living at Amberfields is like crossing the Rubicon. You'll be living the senior life. You are just not ready for that, and you think you'll never be able to cross back."

You'll be living the senior life. The words coursed like thunder through his head. Marion had summed up his fears of Amberfields into a single sentence. Now he could talk about it because he knew she would understand.

"I know that I'm technically a senior citizen, but only chronologically. I don't feel like most of the people inhabiting Amberfields. I don't think like them, and that's what scares me; if I stay here long enough I know I'll change. I'll become just like them. It's inevitable.

"I see Amberfields as an enclave—the same kind of people gathered together surrounded by the real world. It's like the pioneers crossing the prairie, pulling their wagons into a circle to protect themselves from the Indians. But unlike the pioneers, the inmates of Amberfields aren't seeking new horizons. They have banded together to keep the outside world at arm's length."

Max paused, not so much to catch his breath but to choose the right words before he continued. "I want to live out there in the real world, the vital world where people don't have to be fifty-five or older to enter. I want to live where there are children, not just the occasional grandkid that comes to visit but all kinds of kids, neighborhood kids doing noisy kid things because they are the future. I want neighbors of all ages ... from newlyweds to senior citizens. That's the real world, the world where I won't have to trade in my friends, my interests, and most of all, the positive feeling about life that has kept me going since Dorothy's death and strengthened my determination to marry you! When I get to that Rubicon, I'm going to stand on the bank and skip stones across it. That's the way I'll cross the Rubicon!"

Marion listened and understood. She rose from her chair and walked around the table to stand beside Max. He looked up at her as she leaned down and kissed him lightly on the lips. It was their first kiss. He started to rise from his chair, but Marion prevented him. He wanted to return her kiss. He gently pulled her face toward his, but she slid her hand between their faces and put her finger between their lips to prevent them from touching.

"Is something wrong? Why did you stop me?"

"Because I didn't want it to escalate into something we're not ready for ... not here, not now."

"Then why did you kiss me? You must have known how it would affect me."

"I kissed you because I wanted to let you know I understand what you said and that I will be with you wherever you want to go. As far as my kiss escalating into wild passion, it isn't your self-control I'm afraid of. It's mine!"

Max took her hand and kissed it. "There, it's not the passionate kiss I had in mind, just a token until the right time comes along."

"Soon, darling, soon. Now let's watch the movies."

chapter 18

NO SOONER HAD MAX LEFT than the voice started to rant. *Do you realize how close you came to having it happen all over again? And to think, you instigated it.*

"No! No!" Marion shouted. "You're wrong! This time it's different. Now it's real. It can't happen again. Max won't let it."

Max won't let it happen? the voice mocked. *You were lucky this time. Next time you won't be so lucky. And there will be a next time. There always is. Listen to me. Do I have to remind you of how you suffered? Have you forgotten what Carl did to you ... and what you did to him?*

"Please! Please leave me alone," Marion begged. "Let me get on with my life. I don't want to remember that night anymore. I want to forget so I can live again."

You can't forget, Marion. No matter how wonderful you think Max Porter is, he's a man. He will do what men do. He will take what he wants when he wants it! Think, Marion. How many men have you dated since Carl's death? Five? Six? And it always ended the same way. The only thing they wanted was to get you into bed. It won't be any different with Max. He'll start to paw you, and unlike the others, you won't resist because you think he's wonderful and you love him!

"Stop it!" Marion shrieked. "I won't listen to you anymore! Get out! Get out of my head! I won't let you spoil this perfect day."

It won't help. It will happen again. Perhaps not tomorrow or next week, but it will happen.

The voice left Marion with a ringing in her ears. Although she had expected to hear from the voice after Max left, she wasn't prepared for the force of its attack. She was thoroughly exhausted and decided to retire and leave the cleaning up for the morning.

Once in bed, Marion found it difficult to fall asleep. She kept going over the day, savoring the memory of the drive to town, Momma Maria's, and the evening with Max, even the thought of meeting Lone Star. But the voice's words kept intruding, disturbing her reverie. Sleep eluded her until in the small hours she succumbed to exhaustion. She fell asleep only to twist and turn through a dream she had never wanted to dream again. In the dream she relived her last night with Carlton Wade.

chapter 19

S HE HAD WORKED AN EXTRA hour and stopped at the supermarket, and now an hour and a half late she stumbled through the front door, juggling a bag of groceries, her briefcase, an umbrella, and a handbag. It had been one of those days when everything seemed to take forever and didn't work out. Even the supermarket was out of the most important items on her list. She was exhausted. It had been unseasonably cold and had rained on and off for three days. She felt the beginnings of a cold coming on. Now all she wanted to do was get into bed and sleep. She hoped that Carl had made something for his dinner, but knowing Carl's dislike of doing for himself, she doubted it.

Marion unloaded her burdens and threw off her coat. She wondered where Carl had gone. He had no classes scheduled and hadn't mentioned any appointments. There had been no answer when she called to tell him she would be late, so she had left a message on the answering machine. That was more than two hours ago.

She made a cup of tea and sat down at the kitchen table. The hot liquid soothed the soreness that had been building in her throat. As she drank, she thought about Carl and how he had changed. Actually he had started to change ten years before when she had changed jobs and her income had increased considerably. She was now a department manager, the high end of the middle management scale. There was no telling how high up the executive ladder she could climb. She was ambitious, knowledgeable, and highly respected by both senior management and her team.

Carlton Wade, on the other hand, had little to show for his years in academia. It wasn't his credentials. He had been hired as an assistant professor on the strength of his excellent performance as an undergrad and postgraduate student. He was personable and well-liked by his students. He was given tenure, and his colleagues thought that Carl was on the fast track to full professorship. However, his climb from assistant professor to associate professor was slow and tedious. He had been stuck on the fast track for a long time.

Shortly after his promotion to associate professor, Carl met Marion, who was a part-time postgrad in a master's program. They were married after a short engagement, bought a house close to the campus, and settled in. As an associate professor, his salary barely paid the mortgage and taxes on their house. Marion's salary as a well-placed junior executive made up the shortfall and paid all their living expenses. They were very much in love. At least Marion was. She later admitted to herself that she was not quite certain that Carl had ever really loved her.

Only once did they speak of children. Marion thought it was time to start a family, but Carl objected, insisting the time wasn't right. It would be best to wait until he became a full professor. It was a question of priorities, he argued, and his priority was a doctorate, the ticket to full professorship. All his efforts were directed at obtaining that advanced degree. His theme had been chosen and approved, and he spent all his spare time researching and organizing his dissertation. But as the weeks turned into months, Marion noticed that Carl's efforts were slackening. He spent his evenings sitting in his easy chair, reading. He became uncommunicative. He was so removed that there were times when Marion thought he was afflicted by some form of *petit mal* and had slipped into unconsciousness. Sometimes he would awaken from his coma, get into his car, and drive to the local tavern. He never invited Marion to accompany him. When he returned, he acted as though nothing unusual had happened and chided Marion for being concerned. It was evident that they were growing apart. Marion refused to believe that it could be her job that had precipitated the change in Carl, but he was jealous and terribly insecure!

All this was prelude to Marion's night in hell.

Marion finished her tea, rose, and put the cup on the countertop by the sink. She noticed the bag of groceries and searched her memory for anything she had purchased that might require refrigeration. There was nothing, so she decided to leave the bag where it was and empty it in the morning. Carl came through the door just as she was leaving the kitchen to go upstairs to bed. Marion could tell he had been drinking.

He looked at her through half-closed, bleary eyes, "Where the hell have you been?"

"I called to tell you I had some work to finish and then stop at the supermarket to shop. There was no answer, so I left a message on the machine. That was more than two hours ago. I hadn't expected you to be out."

"I couldn't wait for you to make dinner. I went to Barney's for a hamburger."

"And some beer," Marion added.

"Yes, and some beer. I had lots of beer!"

She let that pass. "Well, I'm glad you had something to eat. I've got a miserable cold, and all I want to do is get to bed and try to sleep it off."

She turned and headed out of the kitchen. Carl saw the bag of groceries sitting on the counter and started rummaging through it.

"Did you get any chips?" he shouted after her.

She didn't bother answering him.

Marion dragged herself up the stairs to the bedroom. The stairs were an effort, and she sat on the edge of the bed to catch her breath. She felt feverish. She rose, went into the bathroom, and took two aspirins. There was nothing for her throat so she took another aspirin, chewed it, and swallowed it. It tasted awful but to wash it down with water would defeat its purpose.

She removed her skirt and blouse and threw them into the hamper and returned to the bedroom. After she laid out her nightgown on the bed, she began removing her slip and the rest of her underclothes.

"Very nice. I'd almost forgotten how sexy you look underneath."

She turned and saw Carl leering at her from the doorway. "Not now, Carl. Can't you see I'm ill?"

"You're not ill. It's just another one of your damn excuses!"

Marion picked up the nightgown from the bed, turned, and started toward the bathroom.

Carl stepped in from the doorway. "Don't run away from me, Miss Big Business Executive!" He grabbed her roughly, painfully from behind, spun her around, and threw her onto the bed. "Carl, stop it," she screamed to no avail. He held her down with one hand as the other tore her remaining underclothes away. "You're my wife, and it's about time you fulfilled your wifely duties!" He threw himself on her. She tried to protect herself, but she was too sick, too weak. The unthinkable was happening. Her husband was raping her!

When Carl had satisfied himself, when he had ripped every shred of love she had for him from her body, he cursed her.

"Bitch, things are going to be very different around here now!" he announced as he stormed from the bedroom and the house. Carl never knew how prophetic his pronouncement was.

Marion lay on the bed and cried convulsively. After what seemed an eternity, she rose and went into the bathroom. The mirror confirmed that she was scratched and badly bruised where Carl had attacked her from behind. Her upper body showed the red and purple blotches where his fingers had dug into her. There was a crust of dried blood on her torn lip where he had covered her mouth with his hand to quiet her screams. Her lower body was wet with Carl's slimy ignominy. The sight nauseated her. She leaned over the toilet and vomited Carlton Wade out of her life. *If it were only that easy,* she thought as she pressed the flush lever.

She got into the shower and let the hot water stream over her bruised body, trying to clean away the stains of Carl's attack, but no amount of water could wash away her mental anguish. She had loved Carl with all her heart for so long and this was what she had to show for her love.

Marion felt the effects of her cold intensifying. Her temperature was rising. Her throat burned, and it was becoming hard to breathe. She got out of the shower and toweled off with difficulty. Then after she exchanged the soiled nightgown for a pair of flannel pajamas, she went downstairs and made certain that the windows and doors were locked and bolted. She didn't want Carl to get in when he came back. He could sleep in his office at the college. She climbed the stairs again and headed for bed. Although exhausted, sleep did not come easily, and when it finally did, it was angry and strained.

Marion slept away what was left of the night. When she awoke, she was groggy, and every part of her body ached. Forcing her eyes to focus, she read 9:25 on the bedside clock. As she reached for the phone to call the office, she remembered it was Saturday. The office was closed.

Marion fell back onto the pillow. She wanted to go back to sleep, but there were things she had to do first. With the doors and windows locked and bolted, there was no way that Carl could get back into the house, but she wanted to make certain. With great effort, she rose from the bed and headed for the bathroom. She splashed her face with cold water, and without drying off, she looked into the mirror above the sink. Reflected back was a face suffering the ravages of her cold and the emotional scars of Carl's aggression! She had the weekend to shake the cold. Could the emotional scars ever be erased?

Marion washed, combed her hair, and put on a fresh pair of pajamas. Still feeling chilled, she donned a quilted housecoat and headed downstairs to the kitchen. She put up water for tea, and while she was waiting for the water to boil, she drank a large glass of orange juice.

Suddenly the front door chimes sounded. Marion made no effort to go to the door. The water boiled, and she poured it into a cup. The chimes sounded again, and after a few seconds there was a rapping on the door. Marion could no longer ignore it. She went to the living room and called out through the closed door, "Go away, Carl! You're not coming in! Not after last night!"

Marion heard a woman's voice on the other side of the door say, "Mrs. Wade, this is Police Officer Carla Ludwig. Please open the door. I need to talk to you."

Reluctantly Marion opened the door, and Officer Ludwig entered. Without being obvious, she looked at Marion and noticed the signs of last night's events—the puffed eyes, the cut lip, all the signs of a battered woman. She knew that according to law she couldn't press the issue unless Marion made a complaint. "Are you all right?" she asked.

Marion was stunned. How could she know about last night? "Aside from this miserable cold, I'm fine. But thanks for asking. What was it you wanted to talk to me about?"

"Is there someplace we could sit?"

"Yes, of course." Marion ushered Officer Ludwig to the living room. When they were seated, she asked, "What is this all about?"

Officer Ludwig hesitated. She was doing a job she was trained to do but one she didn't relish. She hadn't told Marion that she was attached to the SCPD Special Services squad, bearers of bad news to next of kin, and the news she bore was the worst. There just wasn't an easy way to say what had to be said, so Officer Ludwig decided to give it to Marion straight and without preamble. "Mrs. Wade, shortly before 1:00 a.m. this morning, after leaving Barney's Bar and Grill, Mr. Wade, driving at high speed, ran off the road and hit a tree. He didn't survive. The police department is conducting an investigation to find out if he was drunk before he left Barney's and if so, why they let him drive."

Marion took a minute to digest what Officer Ludwig had told her. In a low monotone she slowly said, "He was drunk before he stormed out of here last night." Then she broke down and cried not only for herself but for Carl and his lost potential, for his being mired in the fast track, and for not allowing himself the joy of loving as he was loved. Now it was all lost.

After she made certain that Marion would be all right alone, Officer Ludwig left. A few moments later Marion heard the voice for the first time, and her demon was born. When the voice had finished, Marion was no longer the victim. She had assumed the guilt for Carl's death.

chapter 20

MAX LOOKED AT THE CLOCK for the fifth time. It read 10:30. "She should be up by now," he reasoned. Since he was an early riser, Max thought sleeping past ten o'clock was tantamount to sleeping half the day away. He was impatient to spend as much time with Marion as possible. "She must be up by now," he decided. As he reached for the phone to call her, it rang. Startled, he grabbed the receiver and put it to his ear. "Hello?"

"Good morning, Max."

He heard sleep in her voice. "Good morning, Marion. I wanted to call you, but I was afraid I'd wake you."

"That was very sweet of you, darling."

"You sound tired. Didn't you sleep well?"

Marion couldn't tell Max about her anguished dream, not now, not until she overcame her demon. But she had to tell him something. "Actually I had trouble falling asleep, and you're to blame."

Max was taken aback. "Did I do or say anything wrong yesterday? I hope not. I'd hate to think I did something to upset you."

Marion laughed and said, "Nothing as drastic as that, quite the contrary. You gave me such a perfectly wonderful day yesterday that

I relived it at least a dozen times before I could fall asleep. So you see, you're the reason I slept in and sound a little tired."

Relieved, Max, like a good athlete, followed through. "I plead guilty and throw myself on the mercy of the court. But I must warn you, I don't think I can be rehabilitated. I plan to give you another perfectly wonderful day today."

"What did you have in mind? Remember, I just got up. I won't be ready till lunchtime."

"I'll try to survive. We could start by having lunch together."

"I'd like that, but not downstairs. It's too crowded, too noisy. I'd like a quiet place where we can talk and look at each other and even hold hands without the rumor mill shifting into high gear."

"That sounds good to me. Have you any place in mind?"

"Do you like hamburgers?"

Max was intrigued. "Madam, I would have you know that I am a world famous connoisseur of hamburgers. I am also a renowned *chef du hamburger*, having been awarded not one but two Golden Spatula awards from the Old Cronies Neighborhood Barbecue Society."

"My goodness, is there no end to your accomplishments? I hesitate to tell you that I, too, am an accomplished burger flipper. My niece has told me on a number of occasions that if I were to open a hamburger stand near the college, I would become a millionaire. With that said, my proposition to you—"

Max cut in, "Proposition?"

"Oops, I meant to say suggestion. Now stop leering and listen to me. My suggestion is that I prepare a couple of my deluxe hamburger platters and we have a quiet lunch in my apartment."

"You told me your cupboard was bare. Mrs. Wade. Are you trying to seduce me?"

"Oh, stop playing *The Graduate*! My cupboard is bare, but my freezer is full!"

"Oh well, nothing ventured, nothing gained. Can I bring anything?"

"If you have some fresh lettuce and a tomato. I'm afraid my lettuce is wilted and the tomatoes are soft."

"I'll check to see how fresh mine are. How about an antipasto? I have the makings in unopened jars."

"That would be a nice touch. And there's the second bottle of wine we didn't open last night."

"It will be a veritable feast. Who needs Momma Maria?"

Marion answered indignantly, "We do, and you know why, so don't forget it!"

"I do know why, and I think about it all the time. Honey, are we any closer?"

"Yes, darling, very much closer. Now get off the phone so I can get ready."

"By the way, what time is lunch?"

"One o'clock and don't come a minute earlier."

"Somehow I knew you were going to say that."

The simple lunch was a veritable feast. After they finished eating, Max sat back in his chair, and looked across at Marion. He reached across the table. Marion placed her hand in his upturned palm. Nothing was said. They had reached a point of communicating without words. Their eyes said it all.

They sat like this for five full minutes. Max felt the heat build. He had to break the spell before he lost control.

"By the way, we have a date with Lone Star. I spoke to him, and to quote him, he's 'hankering' to meet you."

"Oh, Max! That's wonderful. Can we go this afternoon?"

"You're too anxious. Maybe I'd better reconsider introducing you two."

"Now be serious and don't pout. I like it better when you leer. When are we going to see Lone Star?"

"Tomorrow at lunch, and after lunch you'll get a private showing of *They Call Me Lone Star!* It's all set."

"A private showing just for me? Max, you're amazing!"

"It was easy. Lone Star didn't think he had any fans left, so I didn't have to twist his arm very hard," Max said with a sheepish grin. "So what would you like to do for the rest of the afternoon?" he asked.

"I'd like to walk off this lunch," she replied. "Would you like to walk around the lake?"

Max thought for a moment. "Let's go to Indian Point instead. Lake Manahanik is so much bigger than our little pond. We can walk off our lunch there and then rent a boat and spend the rest of the afternoon relaxing. We can be there in half an hour."

Marion's face lit up. "Do they have canoes?" she asked, "Wouldn't that be fun! I haven't been in a canoe for years."

"That's a great idea! My surprise will be much more appropriate in a canoe."

"What surprise?" demanded Marion.

"It wouldn't be a surprise if I told you, would it?"

"Well, I don't know. The two of us in a canoe ... on the water ... on a lake and then your surprise. It could be dangerous. We could end up *in* the water."

"Not if you control yourself," Max replied, trying to hide his leer.

Marion took his hand and leered right back at him.

chapter 21

THE PARKING LOT WAS ALMOST full. Max drove around looking for an open space closer to the lodge and boat dock, but the only vacant ones he found were at the farthest end of the parking lot. He stopped before he pulled in.

"I think I'll go around again in case a closer spot has opened up."

But Marion was eager to get to the water. "This is fine, darling. We wanted to take a walk before we went out on the lake. From here to the dock qualifies."

"It is a hike, isn't it? But a hike through a parking lot isn't a stroll along a nature trail." Max thought for a moment and then added, "But for romance, a nature trail can't compare with a canoe." He spun the steering wheel and pulled into an open space.

Arm in arm, they walked toward the entrance to the boat dock. Marion glanced down at the package swinging from Max's free hand. It looked like a small knapsack or camera bag. The top was partially unzipped, and a mysterious shape shrouded in green velour protruded through the opening. She assumed it was Max's surprise. She wouldn't put it past him to bring wine and cheese and French bread to highlight the romantic outing.

"Is that your surprise?"

"As a matter of fact, it is," he responded. "I will produce it when we are well underway."

"Outside the twelve-mile limit, I hope," she said, harkening back to the prohibition era when spirits were legal on board a ship when it was twelve miles from shore. She wondered if Max had seen the sign warning that alcoholic beverages were allowed only inside the lodge.

"Don't push it, lady," he admonished. "You can't wheedle the surprise out of me until I'm ready to produce it. And when I do, I guarantee you will be speechless with delight!"

"Aye, aye, captain," she said and laughed. "I surrender!"

They reached the dock where Max rented the last available canoe. It was a broad-beamed vessel with wooden slatted seatbacks. It looked heavy and hard for one person to handle, but to Max's surprise, it sat high in the water and glided effortlessly with the lightest stroke of the paddle. Max reversed the amidships seatback so Marion could face him. He took the seat in the stern. It wasn't the most romantic situation from Max's point of view. He wanted her next to him, but as he paddled smoothly away from the dock, he saw the look of contentment on her face and was satisfied that he was accomplishing his primary task of making her happy. The surprise would be icing on the cake.

Max paddled toward the center of the lake. After a few minutes he decided they were far enough out, so he put the paddle down and let the canoe drift. "And now it's showtime!" he said as he reached down and brought up the case from between his feet. He unzipped the top and withdrew the green velour bag. It wasn't the wine that Marion had expected. Max undid the drawstring and very slowly, for effect, withdrew a ukulele. Marion exploded with laughter.

"You're going to serenade me," she said between gasps. "I love it!"

"I offer a well-rounded courtship using tried and true methods. When the circumstances call for a serenade, I am prepared to serenade, and not with just any song but one that has a very special meaning."

Max put the ukulele down beside him, reached into the case, and brought out a cardboard tube. He removed the endcap and shook out a rolled-up piece of sheet music, the kind that was popular back in the days before TV when people stayed home and sang around the piano. He unfurled it and held it up so Marion could see the cover.

"Sweet Leilani," she exclaimed. "Oh, Max, it's fantastic. Wherever did you find it?"

"At Cinemabilia. Actually it's a present to you from Lone Star. You can thank him personally tomorrow. Now open it up and hold it with the music facing me. I'm okay with the lyrics but a little rusty with the chords."

She was so excited she found herself trembling and had difficulty holding the paper still. Max looked up from the music and said, "Steady, girl. You are about to be serenaded."

He riffed through a few chords, swung into the introduction, and then broke into song. His voice was mellow yet strong, somewhere between a tenor and baritone. He was an old-fashioned crooner, the kind that made love songs sound personal. Crooners sang to hundreds, even thousands over the radio and in movies, yet every woman thought they were singing only to her. Max was singing only to Marion because she was the only woman he loved and who loved him in return.

Sweet Leilani, (he sang) heavenly flower
Nature fashioned roses kissed with dew
And then she placed them in a bower
It was the start of you.

Sweet Leilani, heavenly flower
I dreamed of paradise for two
You are my paradise completed
You are my dream come true.

The sheet music began to shake so violently that Max lost his place and had to stop singing. He looked up at Marion. She was sobbing. He put the ukulele down across his knees, leaned forward, and took her hand. With his other hand he relieved her of the sheet music and placed it on the ukulele. He wanted to pull her to him, but he was afraid the sudden movement would upset the canoe. Instead he took out his handkerchief, and as he passed it to her, he said, "I'm so sorry, sweetheart, I hope it wasn't my singing. I didn't mean to make you cry."

"Oh, Max, darling, don't you know the difference between crying and tears of joy?" She looked at him through her moist eyes, sunlight reflecting a rainbow of colored sparks back at him, and he basked in their light.

"Your serenade was lovely. I'll remember it always."

"I didn't finish," he said.

"You can finish when we get home. Right now I'd like to go somewhere and be close to you. You're too far away."

"I know just the place, and it's nearby. By the time we get back to the dock, return the canoe, and put this stuff in the car, it will be time for happy hour at the lodge. If you like, we can stay and have dinner."

"And then?"

"Then back home so I can finish my serenade, after which I will go back to my apartment, and you will go to sleep in yours. Remember, tomorrow you meet Lone Star. Okay?"

Marion smiled. "Very much okay," she said.

chapter 22

INDIAN POINT LODGE WAS A rustic, two-story log building with a rocking chair-lined veranda. To its left was the entrance to the beach, bathhouse, and snack bar. To its right was the entrance to the dock and boat rentals. It was from this direction that Marion and Max walked hand in hand toward the entrance to the lodge. They climbed the four steps to the porch, walked past the occupants of the rockers, and then went through the doorway into the lobby.

Indian Point Lodge took full advantage of its name with Native American art displayed on the walls, geometric patterned rugs and decorative tribal artifacts scattered around. Its twisted-wood furniture and long oak bar made the room look like the set of a "B" western movie.

Max led Marion to the bar, where happy hour was in full swing. About twenty patrons were clustered around the bar. Across the room was a group of small tables, only one of which was occupied. Max chose a table away from the bar, and a waitress hurried over to take their order.

They agreed on iced tea. They'd have wine with dinner.

The waitress acknowledged the order and then pointed out the array of hors d'oeuvres that were available at the end of the bar. If they liked, she would make up a selection for two.

Max looked to Marion for approval, which came in the form of a nod. "That would be fine," replied Max. "By the way, what time does the restaurant start serving?"

"The kitchen opens at six, sir."

Max looked at his watch. It was 5:20.

"We would like a table by the window at six. Can you arrange it?"

"I'll inform the maitre d'. He'll notify you when it's ready." She turned and headed to the bar with their drink order.

When the waitress was out of earshot, Max took Marion's hand in his and asked, "Happy, honey?"

Marion smiled and squeezed his hand. "Of course I'm happy, darling. You always see to that."

"Oh?" he questioned. "How do I do that?"

"You know very well how you do that!"

Max hesitated before he said anything in response. He knew why he wanted her to be happy, but he wasn't entirely certain how he had accomplished it. It seemed to be happening without any effort on his part. He knew that her marriage had been unhappy, and he wanted to make up for it. It was as simple as that. Then he remembered Dorothy's letter.

"To paraphrase someone I cared for very much, if you make someone happy, you will also make yourself happy. You will be happy together."

Marion became pensive. "Was that someone your late wife?" she asked.

Max looked away, casting back to that moment when Dorothy asked for his promise, a promise he had thought he would never need to fulfill. "Yes. Just before she died, she made me promise that if I ever met someone I admired and fell in love, I must make that someone as happy as I had made her. It would pain Dorothy terribly if she knew that I was lonely because I thought I shouldn't or couldn't be happy with anyone else."

Marion now understood why Max had had such a wonderful marriage. "She must have been a very remarkable person, Max. I'm afraid she's going to be a hard act to follow."

"That's nonsense," Max retorted. "She was smart and had a terrific personality and a great sense of humor, but no more than you have. Sure,

I loved her with all my heart, but she's been gone a long time. She's a memory. When you came into my life, something amazing happened. I found I was still capable of the kind of love that a man feels for the right woman. You are that right woman, Marion, and you'll never have to worry about being compared to a memory."

Marion was choked with emotion. She tried to frame a response, but before she could speak, the waitress came with their drinks and hors d'oeuvres. Seeing that she had interrupted something very personal, she quickly placed the order on the table and went on to another customer.

Marion had regained her composure. She lifted her glass and held it out, waiting for Max to raise his. When he did, they spoke almost in unison, "Cheers," except Marion added, "Darling," and Max said, "Sweetheart." They smiled at each other and sipped their drinks and nibbled the hors d'oeuvres.

The maitre d' appeared. Their table was ready. Max left a tip for the cocktail waitress, and carrying their iced tea, they followed him to their table. After he seated them, the maitre d' informed them their server would arrive to take their order, and then he returned to his station.

Marion was impressed. "Aside from its Death Valley décor, it's pretty spiffy, with a maitre d' in tux, waitstaff in burgundy with gold piping, and busboys looking like hospital orderlies. How is the food?"

Max couldn't help smiling at Marion's assessment. "The owners are trying to create a country club atmosphere. As far as the food is concerned, it's no Momma Maria's, but it's pretty good."

The server came and deposited menus and pushed for another round of drinks, but Max said they would order wine when they decided what they were going to eat. Thus rebuffed, the server bowed obsequiously and backed away, pledging to return when they had made their selection.

Marion looked out the window. The light had changed as the sun had moved farther to the west. The harsh glare of the afternoon was gone, and now the light had softened, covering the lake with a warm, golden patina. The ripples created dancing flecks of opalescent color, captivating her. *It's so lovely,* she thought, afraid to speak for fear of disturbing the moment.

Max watched Marion as she looked at the lake. "It is beautiful at this time of day," he said. Marion turned toward Max. He saw that her eyes were misted and had a faraway look. Something important was occupying her mind. He took her hand and said, "A penny for your thoughts, sweetheart." He had no sooner said the words before regretting having spoken them. They were hackneyed, and he felt they were an incursion into her private thoughts.

The spell was broken but only temporarily. In the few moments between her gazing out the window and turning back to Max, Marion had assayed her relationship with this man whose thoughts seemed to be only of her. He knew of her unhappy marriage. He even knew she had a demon, yet he didn't pry, knowing she would tell him when she was ready. She was very much in love with Max Porter, and she wanted to make him as happy and content as he was making her. Their relationship, she recognized, was pure and honest. Her guilt and the demon be damned, she was not going to lose him!

"Darling, would you mind having a light cold dinner?"

"Not at all," Max replied. "I was thinking along those lines myself. Would a green salad and some cold shrimp or crab and a half bottle of Chardonnay be okay?"

"Perfect. You order, and I'll go and repair my makeup." As she stood to leave the table, she looked at Max. "Darling, I want you to know that you are one of the world's good guys, and I love you very much." Before he could answer, she turned and headed for the ladies' lounge.

When she returned, she looked radiant. Max saw no change in her makeup except a dab or two around her eyes. He knew that makeup had nothing to do with the sparkle in her eyes. That came from deep within her ... from her heart. He wanted to say something appropriate, something profound about their relationship, but he was speechless. Then he realized that it was Marion who had something to say, and Max hoped it was what he longed to hear.

Marion took a deep breath. "Max, darling, I've been doing a lot of thinking, and I've come to the conclusion that I can't risk losing you. So could we get married right away?"

Max wanted to jump up and take her in his arms. Only his dislike of public displays prevented it. Instead, using a great deal of restraint, he casually asked, "Does this mean we are officially engaged?"

"I hope so," she replied.

"Well, in that case—" He reached into his jacket pocket and withdrew a small velour-covered box, opened it, and took out a beautifully set blue-white diamond engagement ring. He took her hand, placed the ring on her finger, and lifted her hand to his lips. "It's official now," he said.

"It's official," Marion whispered. She was overcome with emotion. The tears started to flow.

"Tears of joy?" he asked.

"Yes, darling, tears of joy," she replied.

Max watched as Marion lifted her hand to inspect her ring. She twisted her hand this way and that, watching the light reflect off the stone. "Like it?" he asked.

"Like it? Max, darling, I love it! I never had an engagement ring."

"Why was that?"

"Carl didn't believe in jewelry. Whatever I had, I bought for myself."

"Poor man. He never knew the pleasure of giving. I was on cloud nine watching you when I gave you the ring."

"I'm so glad you feel that way. Carl was different." Marion reflected. "Oh, it wasn't entirely his fault. He was so insecure. I had outdistanced him. My career had taken off. His had stalled. It was very difficult for him."

"We won't ever have to worry about anything like that. I know we'll never compete with one another."

"Never!" she confirmed.

Max reminded her, "Tomorrow we see Lone Star at one o'clock for lunch. If we leave for Summit City early, say about eight, we can be at the Hall of Records by the time it opens. Shouldn't take long to get the license. Tonight I'll call Jim Warner, who happens to be a lodge buddy and my GP. He'll do the blood tests. I'll also call Gerry Ohlsen tonight. I'd like him to officiate."

Marion was surprised to hear the name. "You mean Mayor Gerald Ohlsen? You're going to ask him to marry us?"

"Of course. We're old friends. He would be offended if I didn't ask him."

Marion shook her head and said *sotto voce*, "Lodge buddies, doctors, old friends, even a mayor. Will wonders never cease?"

Max's heart was pounding. His adrenalin was flowing. He was fired up! "We'll have to make a list of the people we want to attend. We'll need it for Momma Maria. Figure about thirty-five. That is about all Momma can accommodate. Can you think of anything else?"

"Lots of things, but we'll have to work out all the details. Let's have dinner and then head home. Remember, we're leaving at eight tomorrow morning."

"Honey, I just thought of something. Which of our two apartments are we going to keep? I vote for yours. It's nicer than mine."

Marion smiled and took Max's hand. "That will be fine for a little while, but as soon as we're married, we'll start looking for a house in the city, something in or near your old neighborhood."

Max was dumbstruck. He hardly knew how to respond. Finally he calmed down enough to ask, "You would leave paradise for the city?"

"Of course I would. Paradise is anywhere we're together. I remember what you said about Amberfields being an enclave designed to keep the real world, the vital world out. I want us to live in the vital world."

"Sweetheart, you are extraordinary, and I love you very much!"

"You are pretty stupendous yourself, and I love you very much too!"

The server came with their dinner. The simple dinner was happily devoured in between conversation. By the time they finished their coffee, the sun had set, and the lake was awash in the hazy blue-green colors of twilight. It was a perfect finale to the day.

chapter 23

THEY WERE ON THE ROAD by 8:15. Traffic was still heavy with stragglers from the earlier morning rush of commuters, and Max was apprehensive. They had taken Marion's Mercedes 380SL with Marion driving. Max's apprehension didn't last long. She was an excellent driver. She knew exactly what to do and when to do it, and she did it well. He sat back and relaxed, realizing that he would never have to worry about her when she was on the road alone. She could take care of herself behind the wheel. The thought satisfied him, and a broad grin spread across his face.

"You're very quiet this morning," she said, turning momentarily toward him, "and what is that grin about?"

"Keep your eyes on the road, or I won't tell you."

"Eyes dead ahead on the road, captain. Now tell me."

Max was still smiling. "If you must know, you've just shattered one of my male ego mind-sets."

"And which one was it? You must have many."

"We'll discuss that last bit another time. I was referring to my previously held false opinion of women drivers. Your handling of the wheel is professional. Your ability with a five-speed manual transmission is so smooth it's awe-inspiring. Oh yes, and your footwork with the clutch is a ballet of coordination."

"So you were looking at my legs?"

"The situation did present itself."

"Darling, you're insane! Will you marry me?"

"Are you proposing to me?"

"Yes, I'm proposing."

"Too bad. I proposed to you first."

"I'll accept your proposal if you'll accept mine. Deal?"

"Deal!"

That settled, they drove on toward Summit City. They were rarely silent. They loved to hear each other's voices and always found reasons to converse.

Once in Summit City, Marion made for city hall. Max directed Marion to a driveway marked, "Official Business Only," and told her to pull in. She started to protest but gave in. Knowing Max, he could turn their quest for a marriage license into official business. The entrance was barred by an automatic barrier. Max handed her a magnetic key card, which she inserted into the lockbox. The barrier swung up, and she drove down a ramp to the underground garage. At the bottom Max directed her to an area marked, "Committee and staff," and pointed out a place to park.

Handing the card back to Max, Marion said, "I'm impressed. You do know people in high places."

Max laughed "All the way to the stratosphere. Actually I'm still a committeeman. There's no residence restriction in Summit City, so instead of resigning when I exiled myself to Amberfields, I took a six-month unpaid leave of absence. After we settle down, I'd like to resume my activities."

"After we're married, we'll be returning to Summit City. You'll be a lot closer to your activities," she reminded him.

"Sweetheart, if there weren't a hundred security cameras looking at us, I'd put my arms around you and give you a big kiss."

At the thought of being observed by the security cameras, Marion blushed and said, "Just hold that thought till we're out of camera range."

Max guided her to the elevator, and they were whisked to the fifth floor and the marriage license bureau. It was early, and they were the only applicants. Behind the counter an older middle-aged civil servant was busy doing clerk things with an automatic date stamp and a sheaf of papers. She looked up and saw two people approaching the counter. There was only one function of this office and the clerk thereof, so there was no need to ask if she could help them. Automatically she handed them a freshly dated application and ticked off the requirements for obtaining a marriage license. This she did automatically, the result of nearly thirty years behind this same counter. She pointed to the table at which they could complete the application. Then it should be returned to her at the counter. It was all very efficient, all very impersonal.

"Thank you, Mrs. Monagham. You've been very helpful," Max said.

A surprised Mrs. Monagham looked up at the two people standing across the counter. Slowly their faces came into focus, and she recognized Max.

"Oh, Committeeman Porter, please forgive me for not recognizing you immediately. If there is anything I can do for you."

Afraid Mrs. Monagham would ramble on forever, Max interjected, "Yes, Mrs. Monagham, there is. How does one obtain a waiver of the waiting period?"

"Obtaining a waiver is somewhat complicated. One has to make application for the waiver, which goes to a judge for review."

"Is there anyone other than a judge who can issue a waiver?"

"Oh, yes, Mr. Porter, the mayor can also issue a waiver."

"I see," Max said. "Then when we complete this application, would you get Mayor Ohlsen on the phone for me?"

"I'd be delighted, Mr. Porter."

The marriage license application was straightforward, and they had no problem filling in the blanks. They returned to the counter and handed Mrs. Monagham the application and their individual identifying material as requested.

"Would you please put through the call to Mayor Ohlsen now?" Max requested.

Mrs. Monagham picked up her phone and pushed the interoffice button and then the mayor's extension.

"Good morning, Mayor Ohlsen's office."

"Hello, Mary? This is Martha Monagham from the marriage license bureau. I have Committeeman Porter here. He would like to speak with the mayor. Okay, I'll hold." A moment later she handed the phone to Max.

"What's up, Max? Got a problem with the license?" Gerry Ohlsen asked.

Now that he had Gerry on the phone, Max realized he didn't really have a legitimate reason to ask for the waiver. "No problem, Gerry. Mrs. Monagham has been very helpful. However, I was wondering if we could get a waiver of the waiting period. I understand you could help in obtaining the waiver."

"Given a legitimate reason, I can issue a waiver on the spot. Do you have a legitimate reason, Max?"

Max tried to come up with a reasonable explanation, but the best he could do was, "Will logistics do?"

Gerry laughed. "That's about as good as any. Okay, Max, you've got it. Put Mrs. Monagham on."

"Thanks, Gerry. We'll see you at the wedding."

"You'd better ... since I'm officiating."

Max handed the phone to Mrs. Monagham. He watched as she nodded her head in acknowledgment of the mayor's instructions. Twenty minutes later she handed Max the marriage license embossed with the great seal of Summit City, a copy of the waiver, and a bill for thirty-five dollars for the license and twenty-five dollars for the waiver to be paid in cash (no checks or credit cards).

The elevator deposited them back at the parking level. Marion was laughing. Max had a confused look on his face.

"I can't believe it!" he said, "Thirty-five dollars! The last time I bought a marriage license, it was three dollars."

Marion contained her laughter long enough to ask, "Don't you think it was worth it? Be careful how you answer. You might have to walk home!"

"Of course it was worth thirty-five dollars. I was just caught up in the changing values."

Marion became serious. "What changing values?"

"Back when marriage licenses were three dollars, uncontested divorces were three thousand dollars or more. Now licenses are thirty-five dollars, and if you believe the ads in the newspaper, divorces are as low as 125 dollars. It just doesn't seem right. If this trend continues, a marriage license will cost 125 dollars, and divorces will cost thirty-five dollars. What will that do to the institution of marriage?" He was still shaking his head, and Marion was still laughing when they drove out of the garage and headed for the office of Dr. James Warner.

chapter 24

WITH THEIR MARRIAGE LICENSE TUCKED away in Max's pocket and Band-Aids covering the sites where their blood had been taken, Marion, following Max's directions, drove to meet Lone Star. They found parking in front of his store, an unusual occurrence. On the window the stylized projector, its neon reels appearing to spin, flashed *Cinemabilia*. Max held the door for Marion, and she entered into a film aficionado's heaven. Every inch was filled with posters and photos, books and projectors, tapes and DVDs along with movie oddments of every kind. As Marion looked around, Max called out, "Hey, Lone Star, I brought your one and only fan. Come on out and say hello."

A voice from the back room drawled an answer, "Well, that's right neighborly of yuh, pardner. I'm beholden to yuh."

Marian recognized the drawl. It was as strong and exciting as it had been when she last heard it many years before. She turned in the direction of the voice. The curtain separating the back room from the store parted, and Lone Star ambled in a few feet and stopped for effect. His timing was perfect. His audience was captivated.

He was attired in the same outfit he made famous in the Lone Star films—the sand-colored broadcloth shirt embellished with filigree embroidery, the red bandana knotted on the left side with its peak loosely draped over his right shoulder, the tan twill trousers tightly tapered into brown leather boots tooled and polished to a metallic shine. His hands hung down within easy reach of his twin six-shooters, held in tooled and studded holsters slung from a bullet-laden gun belt that hugged his hips. The effect was dramatic. Once again Marian was swept into a time warp.

Lone Star reached up and grasped the brim of his ten-gallon Stetson from the back, cowboy style, to avoid snagging the chin cord. He swept it forward and down past his face, to rest at his side in salutation. The move revealed his full crop of gray-streaked black hair, and with his deep brown eyes fixed on Marion, he called to Max, "And you, sir, are you not going to introduce me to this most charming lady?"

Max fell right into character. "My apologies, pardner. I plumb forgot that you had not made the acquaintance of my friend and neighbor, Marion Wade."

He turned to Marion. "Standing here before you, Marian, in all his famous and trademarked regalia is Dave Benjamin, AKA Lone Star, hero of the big and little screen's innumerable "B" westerns that you so admired in your callow youth." Turning to the cowboy, he said, "Lone Star, may I present Marian Wade, the most charming lady you have already made note of and, by some strange quirk or lack of judgment, a long-time admirer of you and your films."

Poor Max, he could hardly keep from laughing, Marion thought. Now it was her turn to assume a role, and she chose the same Southern belle she had used when she met Max in the mail room. "Well, I do declare I am overwhelmed, Mr. Lone Star. If you will permit me to mention it, I would like to state that I am one of your most ardent fans, having seen all your films, some of them two or three times, and now to see you in person, it is indeed an honor, sir, to make your acquaintance."

"Little lady, the honor is all mine," Lone Star said with a gracious bow. Then he turned to Max and asked, "And you, sir, where have you been hiding this lovely lady?" Marion sensed that Max was becoming uncomfortable. Perhaps the little scene they were performing had gone far enough. She left the Southern belle character and returned to herself. "Max told me that we are going to see *They Call Me Lone Star* this afternoon. It's one of my favorites."

Dave shook off his movie persona. "Mine too," he admitted. "It was very much unexpected and the start of a long career in the saddle."

"Is it true that you didn't know how to ride a horse before you became Lone Star?"

Dave laughed. "That sounds like Max has been giving away my trade secrets. Actually what I told Max was that before I left New York, the closest I ever came to a horse was when I asked a mounted cop in Times Square for directions. But by the time I arrived in California, I was a fairly competent horseman. It happened so long ago I seldom think about it now." He paused in thought and then continued, "Look, let me close up, and we'll go back into my apartment. You and Max can get comfortable while I get out of this outfit."

Dave's apartment consisted of four large rooms with a private entrance onto the adjacent street. Dave seated his guests and then headed to his bedroom to change out of his Lone Star costume.

Max looked at Marion. She glowed with a radiance that could only come from happiness deep within. He contented himself with the knowledge that he was responsible for that happiness, although he grudgingly admitted to himself that Lone Star had made a small contribution.

"He's fascinating," Marion offered with emphasis. "He's aged well. He must be in his eighties, but he's still as handsome as I remember from his films."

"He's okay," Max said.

"Why, Max, darling, I believe you *are* jealous."

Dave returned, now in mufti. He had changed to a beautifully tailored chocolate brown suit cut western-style and embellished with welting and piping, a yellow embroidered silk shirt, and a black string tie with a silver and turquoise slider. On his feet were a pair of handsomely tooled oxblood-toned boots. "Much better," he reported. "I'm about due for a new outfit. I must be putting on a little weight."

"Do you get to wear your outfit often?" Marion asked.

"I wear it at civic affairs like the Thanksgiving and Christmas parades and when I attend a film convention. I attend four or five a year."

"Film convention?" Marion asked. "What does one do at a film convention?"

"Mostly watch classic silent and early sound films. Buy, sell, and trade films and memorabilia. Then there are the celebrities, of which I am one. We sign autographs, answer questions, and give interviews to the local press. If one of my films is on the program, I'm asked to introduce it. Max can tell you about the *cons*. We usually go together. As a matter of fact, we first met at a con. It was in seventy-nine or eighty, wasn't it, Max?"

"Eighty-two ... in Syracuse," Max responded.

"Eighty-two— Seems longer ago than that. You sure it was Syracuse?"

"Yep, it was Syracuse in eighty-two, the same year as your current age."

Dave gave in, "Okay, Max. Eighty-two in Syracuse."

Turning back to Marion, Dave enumerated, "Then there's Columbus, Memphis, Los Angeles, and half of a dozen more cons spread out over the year. We don't attend them all, just the main ones."

Max thought this an appropriate time to announce their marriage. Assuming his western drawl again, he said, "Say, pardner, Marion and I are going to get hitched, and we'd like you to be best man."

Dave was not surprised by the announcement. As soon as he had seen Marion, he knew that she was Max's "Sweet Leilani".

"Max, I always knew you were a smart *hombre* and that when you sashayed up to the hitching post, it would be with a thoroughbred filly. I'd be honored to stand up for you."

Marion blushed. Max took her hand and gently squeezed it. Lone Star's approval was akin to getting parental consent.

Dave continued, "Now that it's settled, let's head around the corner to Donahue's Speakeasy and have some of the best bangers and mash this side of the Emerald Isle."

Max turned to Marion. "Honey, you'll love Donahue's. It's done up like a 1920's speakeasy. Drinks are served in teacups just as they were during Prohibition. They used to have sawdust on the floor until the fire marshal made them stop because of the fire hazard. Now the floor is covered with crushed peanut shells. The doorman is on the inside checking you out through a little window in the door. If he knows you or you look all right, he lets you in. Actually he lets everyone in. It's just an act, part of the atmosphere."

"It sounds interesting," Marion responded, "but how's the food?"

Dave answered, "It's good, old-fashioned Irish cooking with aromas and tastes you wouldn't think possible. Tell her, Max."

"What more can I say, Dave? I think you've sold Marion on Donahue's, hasn't he, honey?"

"He certainly has. Now if you two would stop wasting time talking, we could be on our way to Donahue's," Marion replied, and now Dave was introduced to the lilt in her voice that so enthralled Max.

"Yes, ma'am," said Dave.

"I'm ready," chimed Max.

"And then after lunch we'll come back and watch *They Call Me Lone Star* and, if there's time, *The Call of the Coyote*," Dave promised.

"We'll make time, won't we, Max?" Marion asked.

"Certainly," Max responded, "as long as we can hold hands when the lights go out."

"Oh, Max!" Marion chided. "What will Lone Star think of us?"

"I'm sure he'll think of something, won't you, Dave?"

Dave winked at Marion and then said to Max, "I sure will! Right now I'm thinking about bangers and mash at Donahue's. Are you two coming?"

chapter 25

MARION FOUND DONAHUE'S ABSOLUTELY ENCHANTING. She had seen enough old movies on the Turner Classic Movie Channel to recognize the details of a speakeasy. So perfectly had the ambience been designed that she felt she was back in the Prohibition era, drinking bathtub gin from a teacup while the strains of Ruth Etting singing "Ten Cents a Dance" and Helen Morgan lamenting how she "Can't Help Loving Dat Man" poured from the jukebox. Marion kept looking over her shoulder for the police raid, which, according to the movies, should happen any moment now.

The waiter appeared. Dave asked Marion and Max, "Bangers and mash and a schooner all around?"

Although Marion had heard of bangers and mash, she had no idea what they were except that they sounded heavy. She really just wanted something light like a Waldorf salad. Instead she joined in the adventure. "Bangers and mash all around," she confirmed. Turning to Dave, she asked, "What is a schooner?"

Dave was quick to reply, "Just think of it as a large glass of beer. It goes well with bangers and mash."

When their order was deposited before them, Max and Dave, knives and forks in hand and emitting grunts of anticipation, proceeded to attack the contents of their plates. Marion surveyed hers and wondered how anyone could ever eat so much food. Her plate held a mountain of mashed potatoes down which a lava flow of rich and creamy brown gravy cascaded to puddle around the perimeter of the plate. Positioned at the four points of the compass, four sausages—the bangers she assumed—were placed to prevent the mountain from sliding down into the lake of gravy. It was very artistic, though Marion noticed that both Max and Dave's plates had already been reduced to a logjam of sausages floating on gravy-drenched potatoes. But from the expressions on their faces she knew they were relishing their meal.

It wasn't the presentation, she thought, so it had to be the flavor. She speared a banger with her fork and laid it down at the base of the potatoes. Thinking of Max's club sandwich, she cut a bite-sized piece of the sausage, slathered it with some potato, and tentatively put the fork into her mouth. The texture and spices of the banger combined with the silky smoothness of the gravy-laden potatoes created a taste that wiped out any concern she may have had for calories, fats, carbohydrates, or any other unhealthy regimen. She had no trouble finishing off most of her meal.

She was caught in another time warp, courtesy of Max Porter, with whom her life had become one big, captivating adventure. The past, present, and future all merged into a wide screen, Technicolor, beautiful love story. It wasn't the love she had known before, the love she had thought would last forever, the love that had turned to dust. This was Max's love, and now she had the maturity to understand and appreciate it.

The coffee came and lifted her from her reverie. She heard Dave ask if she still wanted to hear about his learning to ride a horse and how he became Lone Star.

"It's a long story," warned Max.

"Don't worry," countered Dave. "I'll try to make it short so we can get back to see the films."

"Don't make it too short, Dave," Marion insisted. "I want to hear all about your odyssey from the Bronx to Hollywood. Remember, I'm your number-one fan."

Dave thought for a moment. "Marion," he said, "I certainly appreciate your being my number-one fan, but telling the whole story might take an hour or more. So while we finish our coffee, let me give you a synopsis of how Dave Benjamin from the Bronx, New York, became Lone Star of Poverty Row, Hollywood. It shouldn't take more than a few minutes of well-chosen sentences, and then we'll have plenty of time for at least one Lone Star film. After you two are married, we'll have a Lone Star film festival, and I'll narrate my odyssey in all its glorious detail between films."

"Honey, I think we should accept Dave's offer. Once he gets started, we'll be here all evening and not get to see *They Call Me Lone Star.*"

Marion feigned a pout and demanded of Dave, "You promise?"

"I promise, Miss Marion, and I'm most beholden to yuh," replied Lone Star.

Dave, the consummate actor, cleared his throat for effect, and using his New York accent, he began, "I was an actor in New York. But those were bad years on Broadway, and I was having a hard time finding work. Even though television production was centered in New York at the time, there weren't many good acting jobs available, so I decided to try Hollywood.

"I bought a bus ticket and got bored after the first day, so I decided to hitchhike. There weren't as many loonies on the roads back then, so it was much easier to get rides. I wound up visiting a lot of places and meeting a lot of interesting people, many more than I would have met on a bus. For an actor it was a good learning experience. I took odd jobs to support my eating habit and never had trouble finding work. I bussed tables, mowed lawns, even filled in for a sick fry cook for a week. I got to Phoenix and found a job as a cook's helper on a ranch. It was there I learned to ride a horse and correctly wear western clothes. After six months I decided it was time to move on.

"When I got to Hollywood, the only work I could get was as an extra in a Poverty Row company that produced horse operas. I figured it wasn't any worse than bussing tables or being a fry cook in a greasy spoon. Something better would come along. My first day in front of the camera could have been my last if the producer hadn't been on the set.

"My part called for me to stand with a group of six other cowhands who had just captured a group of rustlers. The ranch foreman was hell-bent for a hanging, and his line was, 'Let's show these varmints some range justice.' Then he pointed at me—I was the closest—and said, 'You, thar, git yur rope over that thar tree limb.' I saw an opening for padding my part with a little improvisation. While the foreman was spitting out his orders to me, I fixed him with a steely-eyed stare and slowly, emphatically drawled out, 'They call me Lone Star.'

"All hell broke loose! The director shouted, 'Cut!' The actor playing the foreman rushed over and wanted to deck me, but he changed his mind when he saw my clenched fists. Then the producer called out, 'Print that!' He and the director went into a huddle, and after a few minutes he came over and asked my name, my real name. I told him, and he said to come back to his office with him. He sent the company home and told them to report back in two days. That's how long it took to write the script for *They Call Me Lone Star*. The producer was a sharp character who was also from New York named Chick Young. He told me that all the 'B' westerns were made by the Poverty Row companies and that there was fierce competition between them for distribution. When I adlibbed the Lone Star line, Chick saw a whole series of films revolving around Lone Star, and he wanted me to play the role. The rest you know."

Dave's narrative had taken less than five minutes. Marion had been glued to Dave's every word, visualizing his history in her mind's eye, living his adventure. Now she recognized the strength of this man and understood why as a young girl she was so taken by him and his Lone Star character.

"Now let's head back and watch a film," Dave said as he paid the check.

chapter 26

TEN MINUTES LATER THE THREE were back at Dave's apartment in what he called his study, a comfortably furnished room filled with film memorabilia. The projector was set up at one end of the room, the screen at the other. Marion and Max were appropriately seated on a love seat facing the screen. Dave was tending to the projector, getting it ready for the film showing.

Marion took Max's hand and squeezed it. "I can't believe this is really happening. I'm actually going to see *They Call Me Lone Star* again. Thank you, darling, for making it all happen."

"Just more of my friendly customer service," he replied.

The lights dimmed, and Dave called from beside the projector, "If you two love birds are through billing and cooing, the main feature starts in ten seconds."

Now it was Marion's turn to be ten years old. She squealed with delight as the main title filled the screen. Reaching over, she took Max's hand and guided his arm around her shoulder and then snuggled up to him. Now everything was perfect. She was seeing a film she thought she would never see again with the man she loved above all else.

The titles were printed over a montage of constantly changing action scenes from the film. After the last title card was displayed, the scene in the center expanded outward to fill the entire screen. Lone Star was leading a posse on the heels of escaping bank robbers. The camera cut to a close-up of Lone Star leaning forward in the saddle, grim, determined, and, Marion thought, very handsome. This was the Lone Star she remembered, the play-acting Lone Star. Now she also knew the real Lone Star, Dave Benjamin. Lone Star and Dave were one and the same. Only the years separated them.

Like all "B" westerns, the action was fast, the dialogue slow. Good overcame evil, and time raced by. Sixty-five minutes later the end title flashed on the screen, and the lights slowly came up. Marion sat with Max's arm still around her, her hand holding his, her head now resting on his shoulder. They seemed lost to time and place. They were experiencing that moment of introspection one feels after an emotional event, Marion reflecting on the turn her life had taken since she had met and fallen in love with Maxfield Porter. She was most certainly in love with this man, who had shown her the true meaning of the word. His love was for her alone, and he was not ashamed to show it. No voice or demon could ever stop her from loving him.

Max was also reflecting on how he had consigned himself to an ice floe to drift away from life until he had met Marion Wade, who, by simply calling him Nanook, had saved his life. What he felt for Marion was immediate and much beyond gratitude. In the vast wilderness of Amberfields he had found someone to love.

So much had changed since that morning in the mail room. He saw things differently—the lunch at Momma Maria's, the day at Indian Point, this morning at the license bureau, introducing Marion to Dave.

Max had seen *They Call Me Lone Star* at least fifteen times. The neighborhood kids loved the westerns, and he showed them often. But this afternoon's showing was different. The film seemed more personal, the characters more finely drawn, and the film more than just a "B" western. The explanation was simple enough. When they were together, he saw the world around him through Marion's eyes!

Dave's voice from beside the projector interrupted their reveries. "Do you want to see another *Lone Star*, or have you had enough?"

Max took his arm from around Marion's shoulder, "It's been a long day, honey. Can you handle another one? We still have the drive back to Amberfields."

"You're probably right. It has been a full day, and I am a little tired. How did we manage to cram so much into one day?"

"Full days lead to full lives," Max jokingly philosophized.

Dave left the projector and came forward.

"I'm glad you enjoyed *They Call Me Lone Star*, Marion. It isn't often I get such an appreciative audience."

Marion smiled and said, "I never thought I'd see any of your films again. It's been almost fifty years since I last saw a Lone Star movie. That doesn't include the TV series, of course. I saw most of those through the early sixties."

"I take it you were a fan of western films. There weren't many females that fit that description."

"I don't think it had anything to do with my being female. There was something about your films that was different, something I couldn't define, but whatever it was, it set your films apart from other westerns."

Marion paused for only a brief moment, but that was enough for the answer to reveal itself. "You mentioned earlier, Dave, that in order to pad your part in your first appearance, you improvised, and it worked. It started your career and became part of your persona. Now I know what that indefinable quality was that made your films so spontaneous and unpredictable and *believable*. Tell me, Dave, how much of your films was improvisation?"

Dave didn't answer Marion. Instead he looked at Max and said, "Max, old buddy, I hope you realize that in Marion you have one very exceptional woman." Then to both of them, he continued, "No one outside my small production company knew anything about the improvisation. We kept it a secret. It was never mentioned to the press or the trade papers, yet Marion understood that's what made my films different when all the experts and critics never came close."

"She's something, isn't she?" Max's smile couldn't have been any broader without serious facial damage.

Brushing aside the accolades, Marion continued, "It's true, Dave. You took an overworked genre, the horse opera, and elevated it to an entertaining, well-played series of features. And then there's your TV series, which ran for six years. To thousands of kids and adults, Lone Star was real and important, a bastion of truth and right! And you did this at a time when most other cowboy actors had to sing for their supper and share billing with a horse. As one of your fans and now a friend, I would say that's a real accomplishment."

Dave found it difficult to respond to Marion's great compliment. "I hardly know what to say, Marion. I never considered that what I did as Lone Star was anything more than simple entertainment. Above all, I was an actor, an entertainer, and that was all I did... or ever wanted to do. What did it matter that most of my acting was done from the saddle and my costume so prescribed it became a trademark? I was confident that I could play Cyrano or King Lear if the opportunity presented itself. All it took was acting experience, dedication, and the ability to immerse oneself in the role. These were qualities I possessed. Nothing else ever entered into the equation.

"I appreciate your kind words. As an actor, I revel in words of praise. It's a form of verbal applause, something every actor needs. But when it's spelled out, it surprises me. It implies that I knew what I was doing. As you said, in our films so much was improvised. It worked because we were a group of professional actors playing cowboys and a bunch of cowboys playing actors, a team where everyone did what he did best."

Dave paused and looked at his friends. Their attention was fixed on his story. Their eyes pleaded with him to continue. They wanted more.

Dave continued, "We didn't have much of a script for the first film, so we made it up as we went along. When we saw the rushes everything looked so natural we knew we had achieved a new way of working, and it set the pattern for the rest of the Lone Star films. Chick Young, the producer, was afraid we were going to get arty, but we were having too much fun to spoil the pictures with messages. After the third picture he went back to counting the receipts and left the picture making to us."

"What wonderful memories. You must have lots of good stories about your time in Hollywood," Marion exclaimed. "We'd love to hear some more of them, wouldn't we, Max?"

"It hurts me to agree, but I would like to hear more. What I want to know is how come you never told me about your Hollywood exploits before?"

"Well, friend," Dave said, winking at Marion, "I didn't think you'd be interested. But now that you have Marion to help you with an appreciation of the finer things in life, I'm sure I'll find some anecdotes to interest you."

"And more films," Marion added.

"You're going to see a lot of films when you two are married," Dave said. "At last count Max had over three hundred feature films and hundreds of shorts in his collection, all first-quality prints. You may not have time for anything else. Now I have an announcement to make. I received an invitation to show one of the Lone Stars at Syracuse. I can select the title and not only introduce it but give a little talk on the making of the Lone Star films. I might even include something about our improvisation. It'll be fun for you, Marion. You'll be attending your first con."

chapter 27

JEANNE'S PLANE WAS ON TIME. Five minutes later it was at the gate, and the passengers were deplaning. As Jeanne came down the ramp, she saw Robert waiting by the carrousel that displayed her flight number. She waved, and he responded with a slight lift of his hand. She did not expect more of an acknowledgment. Like his father, he disliked public displays of emotion. Regardless of that, she came up beside him and kissed his cheek. "It's good to be home. Did you miss me?" Before he could answer, the carrousel began to clank and move as baggage tumbled out of the chute onto the belt. After a dozen bags slid past, Robert recognized one as Jeanne's and whipped it off the moving belt. Bag in hand, he turned to Jeanne and said, "Welcome home," and led the way to their car.

Jeanne felt uneasy. She was reluctant to tell Robert about the job offer. She sensed that to spring it on him while he was driving home would be a mistake. It needed a preamble, a buildup so that he would see the benefit of relocating to the West Coast. It could wait until they got to their apartment, where, she thought, the time and the surroundings would be more favorable. She was certain he could be convinced. She had methods that had always worked with Robert.

Robert was also reluctant to talk about his appointment as vice president. It was official now, replete with a new office with his name emblazoned on the door, two assistants, and staff in adjacent offices as well as a contract that guaranteed a very large raise in salary and stock options along with assorted perks. In the history of the company no one under fifty years of age had ever achieved this elevated position. He mentally patted himself on the back. He was only forty-one.

Under normal circumstances he would have found it difficult to keep his good fortune from Jeanne. He would have wanted to share it with her, and afterward they would have celebrated. But these were not normal circumstances. He knew that she did not go to San Francisco for American Paragon but instead to interview for a new job. She had lied to him. He could find no cause for celebration.

Robert wondered when she would start talking about her trip. So far she hadn't said anything about it. He tried to draw her out. "Was your trip successful?"

"Very," she replied. "I was with a group of interesting people, and we kicked around some new marketing ideas. All in all, I think it may have been the most important meeting of my career. And San Francisco is wonderful. There's so much to do and see. It makes Summit City seem so... provincial. You should see it, Robert. You'd love it."

She was beginning her sales pitch, but Robert wasn't buying any of it. "I've been there a number of times," he said without enthusiasm.

Robert was not reacting as she thought he would. He seemed remote, even disinterested. She decided to change the subject. "What have you been doing while I was away? Out all night carousing?"

"Hardly. I've spent the past two days moving into a new office. I'm pretty bushed."

Jeanne became apprehensive. She was afraid Robert had been given a promotion, and that would upset her plans for their relocating to San Francisco. Robert anticipated Jeanne's reaction, and since he didn't want to tell her about his appointment, at least not yet, was quick to add, "I needed more office space, and with my boss's retirement, it was decided some realignment would be possible. We played musical offices, and I got the space I needed. It was as simple as that."

Jeanne couldn't understand what was on Robert's mind. She had never known him to be so reticent, so reserved, so off the point. She realized that her plan had gone awry. Somehow Robert had learned the real reason she had made the trip. It was time for damage control. She had best tell him now and get it over with.

"Robert, about this trip to San Francisco—"

"Not now," Robert snapped. "Wait until we're back at the apartment."

Twenty minutes later Jeanne deposited her bag in the bedroom while Robert hung their coats in the hall closet. They met in the kitchen.

"Would you like a cup of tea?" Robert asked.

Anticipating the coming discussion, Jeanne replied, "I think I'd prefer a drink, if you don't mind."

"Help yourself and pour one for me," he said as she headed to the drink cabinet. She returned with bourbon for him and scotch for herself. With drinks in hand, they went to the living room and sat opposite each other, sipping their drinks, their eyes averted, neither speaking. Finally Jeanne looked up at Robert, "You know, don't you?"

"Yes, I knew before you left."

Jeanne didn't understand. "Yet you didn't question my going?"

"Would it have made any difference? Anyway, I had to find out what you would do if you were offered the job, but more importantly, how you would react if you were rejected."

Jeanne took a sip of her scotch and smiled. "But I wasn't rejected. I was offered the job."

"Congratulations. Did you accept?"

"I have two weeks to think it over. I wanted to discuss it with you."

"Okay, discuss. You first."

Jeanne swallowed half her drink. She was shifting into sales mode, and this would be the most important sale of her career.

"Robert, darling, this job is the opportunity of a lifetime for me. As well as a substantial increase in pay, the perks are considerably better than anything American Paragon has to offer. And the biggest perk of all is that it's a managerial position! I'll be manager of sales for the entire West Coast with a staff of twelve. I figured it out on the plane coming home. I'll be making two and a half times what I'm making now, and that doesn't include the 2 percent overwrite on all sales over a million dollars. I doubt that I could ever achieve this level with American Paragon."

"Sounds like a pretty good offer, but the commute would be a little difficult. How did you plan to work that out?"

"Oh, Robert, please be serious. We'd relocate to San Francisco naturally."

"And without consulting with me, you assumed that I would drop everything and go with you to San Francisco? What would I do there? Start all over?"

"You would get another job. I'm certain there are plenty of jobs available for someone on your level."

"*For someone on my level,*" he shouted. "You haven't the remotest notion what my level is!" Robert could no longer hold back his anger. It was time to set her straight. His tone of voice was unmistakable. "It's quite evident that you have little interest in my work. You are so wrapped up in *your* career that you never considered that I might have a career as well! You think that all I have is a job. At the snap of your fingers I will give up everything I've worked for and follow you across the country because you have to further *your* career and I only have a job! I think it's time for us to look at our respective careers and our marriage and determine how important they are to us because it is clear that our careers are on a collision course! There isn't much time left now that I'm senior vice president of operations."

Pausing, Robert waited for Jeanne to say something, anything to show she understood what he was telling her. She was confused, so she said nothing and just sat, blankly waiting for Robert to continue. After a moment she became aware of Robert's voice. "I'm afraid that you will have to decide whether the position in San Francisco is more important to you than being the wife of a senior corporate executive while still retaining your position at American Paragon. It's your choice, Jeanne."

Jeanne finally snapped back to life. What Robert said had shocked her. This was more than she had bargained for. She never thought it would be she who had to make the choice. After a moment she recovered, "But darling, you don't seem to understand how important this move is to me ... to my career."

"And you, darling, haven't heard a word I've just said, so I had best spell it out for you again so that you can understand why I am unavailable to follow you. I will not give up a vice presidency so that you can take a job on the West Coast, no matter how much that job furthers your career. I will not give up my home, such as it is, my father, my friends, my interests, or my career to follow your pie-in-the-sky dream of grandeur. I can't stop you from taking this job and moving to the West Coast. I can only remind you that our marriage cannot survive with you in San Francisco and me in Summit City. I've made my choice. You have two weeks to make yours."

chapter 28

"WHAT A WONDERFUL DAY," MARION sighed. "I didn't think it was possible to cram so much into one day."

Max, now driving Marion's 380SL, took his eyes from the road and glanced at Marion. She was sitting with her head back against the headrest, reliving the events of the day, savoring them. He returned his eyes to the road. As the car hummed along, he suddenly felt a pang of sadness at the thought that soon they would be back at Amberfields and would have to part, if only for the night. He resented every minute they were not together.

Marion roused herself and asked, "Darling, did you have anything planned for tomorrow?"

Max thought for a moment before he answered. Then he remembered. The day had been so full he had forgotten to mention his plans to Marion. He hastened to correct his oversight. "This morning I called Robert. Jeanne arrived back from San Francisco last night. I invited them to have dinner with us tomorrow evening. Give them a chance to meet their new wicked stepmother. It will be a double celebration— our wedding and Robert's promotion to vice president of operations at Layton Industries. I'm sorry for not mentioning it, but with all the excitement today, I completely forgot."

Marion was thrilled. "It's understandable, darling. I was hoping to meet your son and daughter-in-law before the wedding. That's wonderful news about Robert's promotion. I've done business with Layton Industries. They're a first-class company."

"You know, honey, I just realized that I don't know anything about your career or when you retired. Just what was it you did?"

Marion laughed and said, "If you call loving your work a career, then I had a wonderful career. I retired five months ago from American Paragon as senior vice president of corporate affairs. I'm still on the board, and I'm also called in occasionally as a consultant. Actually I retired early so I could move to Amberfields and find and marry a guy named Maxfield Porter. Now you know my entire history."

"That's some history. I especially like that last part about marrying Max Porter." He thought for a moment and then said, "American Paragon. That's where Jeanne works. Did you know her?"

Marion seemed reluctant to answer. "I was briefly involved with reviewing her performance for a new position within the company. I had to reject her. I felt she had too many issues."

Max was not surprised. "From what Robert has told me, they have a real career conflict," he said.

Marion nodded her head in agreement. Career conflicts were nothing new to her. "Two careers headed in different directions, tugging at each other. Something eventually has to give. It isn't a very promising situation. I've seen a lot of that in my career." *As well as in my own marriage*, she thought. "Under the circumstances I had to eliminate Jeanne from consideration for the new position. There were other issues as well. I'm sure she holds me responsible for her being passed over."

"How do you think she'll react to meeting you tomorrow evening?"

"That remains to be seen," Marion replied. "I'll try to handle it without creating any more problems. That's what you pay me for."

Max laughed at Marion's somewhat flippant remark. "Personally I'm all for letting the kids work out their own problems," he replied.

"That's usually the best approach," Marion agreed, "but sometimes a little third-party direction works wonders, like pointing out alternatives. It can add another dimension. I'll play it as it lays, as they say on the golf course."

Without taking his eyes from the road, Max reached across and took her hand. "Honey, there's something I think you should know before meeting Jeanne." Max told Marion all about Jeanne—her agenda, San Francisco, and the present state of affairs just as Robert had told it to him.

chapter 29

THE FOLLOWING MORNING MAX'S PHONE rang at eight o'clock. He had been waiting impatiently for it to ring. When he picked it up and heard Marion's voice, his day began.

"Good morning, darling. Breakfast in ten minutes," she said.

"It only takes three minutes to get to your apartment. Could I come now?"

"So who's stopping you?" she responded, "You can set the table."

"I'm good at that. I learned when I was a teenager."

"You're still a teenager," she said and laughed. "Hurry over."

Almost from their first meeting in the mail room, Marion and Max had each assumed an almost flippant persona that came about spontaneously. They had found each other and grown to love each other. They felt young again, but their years and experience enabled them to see the reality of their life together. If they took the time to analyze their relationship, they would conclude that they were really one person, both sides of a two-headed coin. But they had no time for analysis. What teenager ever had?

Max had expected the aroma of bacon and eggs to assail his olfactory sensors. Instead he was greeted by the altogether more subtle scent of real old-fashioned oatmeal simmering on the stove and hot buttered toast warming in the oven. His mind flashed back to their first meal together—Marion in the kitchenette, humming as she prepared their omelets while he tinkered with the TV, reveling in the sights and sounds and smells of domesticity. He tried to remember when that had happened. It seemed so long ago, yet it was just a scant few days.

He kissed her good morning. It was a gentle kiss. She responded and then raised her hand to his face and caressed his cheek. It was not easy to hold their passion in check, but they promised themselves not to break the covenant they had tacitly entered into.

Max felt strongly about their relationship. He disliked that word. It was a corrupted word, a word whose meaning had been changed to cover things that were anathema to his time and place. For their situation he preferred the archaic *courtship*, a word defined by commitment, restraint, and respect.

"I'm here to set the table as ordered, ma'am. Cloth or place mats?"

"Place mats."

"Napkins ... paper or cloth with rings?"

"Paper."

"Cups or mugs?"

"Mugs."

"We're very informal today, aren't we?"

"I'm saving formal for dinner."

"It's not going to be that formal. You'll love Robert, and I think you and Jeanne can get along. You do have some things in common."

"I hope so. I wouldn't want to add to their difficulties."

"You'll do fine, honey. I have every confidence in you."

"Thank you, darling. I love you too."

Marion served up the oatmeal and buttered toast. Max poured the coffee.

They consumed their breakfast with conversation. He complimented her on her oatmeal. She applauded his good taste. He told her for the third time this morning that he loved her. She repaid the offering with an air kiss to show him the feeling was mutual.

They finished breakfast, and Max cleared the table. Marion put the dishes into the dishwasher while Max returned the sugar bowl to the cabinet above the counter. Not one "You do" or "I'll do" was said by either of them. They worked in unison with the precision of a long-married couple, neither recognizing the uniqueness of what they were doing and what a wonderful rapport it signified.

When they finished, they sat in the living room, discussing their wedding plans. "All the guests have confirmed," Max reported. "Everyone's coming. Gerry is coming early so he can go over his speech to make sure it's okay with us." He hesitated before he continued. "He offered to marry us this afternoon at his office and repeat the ceremony on Sunday at Momma Maria's. He felt we might want to have our honeymoon over the weekend."

"What did you tell him?"

"I knew he was trying to do us a favor, so I diplomatically told him that I thought it would make the second ceremony anticlimactic and that we didn't want to disappoint Momma Maria."

"How did he take it?"

"Well, I think. All he did was smile and say, 'I should have known.'"

Marion was delighted. "You did the right thing."

Max was glad she thought so. "Thank you."

"I spoke to Momma Maria," Marion reported. "She described the dinner. It sounds wonderful, very continental."

"If I know Momma, it's going to be an outstanding wedding dinner."

"For a very special wedding," Marion said.

They sat quietly for a few minutes, each reflecting on the upcoming day. Finally Max broke the silence, "Is there anything you would like to do before we go to meet Robert and Jeanne?"

Now it was Marion's turn to apologize. "Oh, darling, I forgot to mention it. Edna and I are going shopping for my trousseau. We're leaving at 10:30 and should be back by three in plenty of time for me to get ready for dinner."

"Can I tag along?"

"No, you can't. It's a girl thing."

"I just thought I could help you pick out some things."

Marion laughed. "I have a pretty good idea of what you would pick out. Better it should be a surprise."

"I can hardly wait."

"Well, you'd better! Now get out of here so I can get ready."

chapter 30

WHEN MAX HAD PLANNED THE evening, he'd intended to book a table at Momma Maria's, but he changed his mind in favor of Chez Jean Luc, Summit City's most upscale restaurant. After all, this dinner was in celebration of Robert's appointment as vice president.

Robert and Jeanne arrived early and were seated opposite each other at a table for four. "You have no idea who she is? Didn't your father tell you anything about her?"

"Just that her first name is Marion, that she's a neighbor at Amberfields, a widow, and that they are getting married Sunday and we're invited. I'm sure we'll learn more tonight."

"Well, I certainly hope so. After all, you have to protect your interests."

Robert displayed his annoyance, the edge to his voice undeniable. "Lighten up, Jeanne," he said. "My only *interest* is my father's happiness. Dad is perfectly able to take care of himself. As he told us once before, he's a big boy now. If he wants to get married, so be it. Dad will be seventy soon, and that's a tough age to be alone. I'm happy that he's found someone, and you should be too. He's doing what's right for him, and I'm all for it."

Robert paused, picked up the glass of bourbon that rested near his right hand, and drained it. He looked across the table at Jeanne. She sat there, smarting from Robert's rebuke. He hadn't wanted to hurt her, but he wanted her to understand how he felt about his father. After he put the glass down, he slid his hand across the table and took Jeanne's hand. "Honey, I know you don't think very highly of the male of the species, but we do have some good qualities. We're excellent workers. We're mostly kind and gentle, and given a chance, we make loving husbands and caring fathers. We know what we have to do in this crazy world, and all we need to make it work is a wife who—" He didn't have a chance to finish.

Jeanne was seated so that the entrance to the dining room was in full view. "Oh! No! It can't be!" Jeanne exclaimed. She jerked her hand away from Robert and sat up in her chair, her face ashen.

Robert was startled by Jeanne's sudden outburst. "What's wrong?" he asked excitedly.

"That woman with Max. She's Marion Wade, the Iron Maiden, my nemesis!"

"Nemesis?" Robert swiveled around in his chair, saw his father with a very attractive woman at the entrance to the dining area, and watched as they followed the maitre d' to their table. There was no time for further questions.

The maitre d' held the chair to the left of Robert as Marion seated herself, while Max seated himself opposite. As soon as the maitre d' left, Max announced, "Jeanne, Robert, I'd like you to meet Marion Wade, the future Mrs. Maxfield Porter."

Robert acknowledged her by putting his hand out to Marion. "I'm very happy to meet you, Mrs. Wade."

Marion took his hand. "Thank you, Robert. I've been so looking forward to meeting you. And please ... call me Marion." She turned to Jeanne. "I'm glad to see you again, Jeanne."

Jeanne did not immediately acknowledge Marion's greeting. Instead she looked at Robert and said, "Mrs. Wade recently retired from American Paragon." She turned to Marion and said, "It was about five months ago, wasn't it, Mrs. Wade?"

Before Marion could answer, Robert broke in, "So you two worked together at American Paragon?"

"Well, hardly together," Jeanne responded sharply. "We both worked *at* American Paragon. Mrs. Wade was vice president of corporate affairs. Our paths rarely crossed. But when they did—"

"We met under difficult circumstances," Marion interjected. "I'm afraid Jeanne holds me responsible for her being passed over for a new position." She looked at Jeanne and said, "I'm sorry you've taken my decision personally, Jeanne. I did what was best for the company and for your future with the company."

"You needn't have worried about my future with the company, Mrs. Wade. I've been offered a higher-level position with another company, and I've decided to take it."

Robert was stunned by Jeanne's declaration. "Is that decision final?" he asked.

"It's as final as I can make it," Jeanne replied. She stood up and announced, "I'm going to freshen up. If the waiter comes, order me another scotch." She turned and walked away from the table.

Robert was beside himself. He hadn't expected Jeanne to exhibit such vindictiveness toward Marion. "Marion, please forgive her. She's been so worked up over this job offer. She wants to accept it, but I won't leave my job to go with her. It's a very frustrating situation for her. Meeting you again this evening prompted her to lose control. I'm sure she'll apologize when she calms down."

Max hadn't said anything since he had introduced Marion. He thought Jeanne's reaction to Marion was rude and unforgiveable. "What did Jeanne say when you told her you wouldn't go with her?"

"That's the strange part. I don't think she heard a word I said. She just kept talking about how important the job was to her and how wonderful it was going to be for us in San Francisco. Finally I told her that she would have to make a choice."

Marion said, "Jeanne seems to be in a state of denial. She only heard what she wanted to hear. She feels that in the end you will go with her because it's so important to her. Max, darling, order the drinks while I see if I can set things right." She rose and headed after Jeanne.

Marion entered the ladies' lounge and saw Jeanne sitting at a vanity table, staring into the mirror. As Marion approached, she was startled by Jeanne's reflection. Her skin was pulled tight, her lips two narrow lines stretched tightly across her face. But it was her eyes that were the most disturbing. The lids were drawn up, and two dark orbs glowed as though they were sending a signal to the mirror and back to her brain. Jeanne was reinforcing herself, commanding herself to take charge. She had made her decision, and she wasn't going to be coerced into changing.

Jeanne became aware of Marion's presence. She turned and asked contemptuously, "More lectures?"

"No lectures," Marion replied, "just some questions that have to be asked."

"And the Iron Maiden has appointed herself head inquisitor."

"If you like. This question is one that Robert is certain to ask. You should be prepared. Your abrupt decision to accept the job in San Francisco, was it prompted by my unexpected appearance as your future mother-in-law?"

Jeanne opened her mouth to either answer the question or to protest, but Marion didn't give her a chance. "There's no need to answer now. Just think about the answers, and you'll know how and to whom to answer later on. To continue, Robert has already told you that even though he loves you, he will not give up his job and go with you. Knowing this, why would you give up a loving husband for your name on an office door and a job that you are totally unqualified and untrained for?"

Jeanne exploded! "What gives you the right to judge my qualifications? And as for Robert, when he wakes up to how important this job is to our future, he'll be happy to come with me!"

Marion pressed on. "It's quite evident that you refused to listen to Robert when he told you why he can't go with you. Do you know why we are having dinner together tonight? It's not to introduce me to Max's son and daughter-in-law. That could just as well be done on Sunday at the wedding. It's in celebration of Robert's appointment as vice president of operations, Jeanne, a very senior position. And if you weren't so wrapped up in yourself, you would be overjoyed with pride as his wife."

"I've heard enough," Jeanne snapped. "I'm going to accept the position, and there's nothing more to say."

"You're right. There is nothing more to say, except—" Marion opened her handbag and removed a sheet of paper. "Here is something you should read before you make your decision final." She handed the paper to Jeanne.

"What's this?" Jeanne asked suspiciously.

"It's the agenda for American Paragon's next board of directors meeting. It was faxed to me this morning."

Jeanne looked at the paper and asked, "Why to you? You're retired. What have you to do with the board of directors? And how does it concern me?"

"I've retired only from the workforce. I'm still a member of the board. Now if you'll read item number one of the agenda, I think you'll understand."

Marion watched as Jeanne unfolded the paper. "Read it aloud," she instructed. "I want to make sure you understand it."

Jeanne began to read haltingly at first, dwelling on each word as though she were proofreading for punctuation and spelling, and then faster as she realized the individual words were meaningless, that the meaning was in the sum total of the words. "Agenda item number one," she read, "review of acquisition committee report Re: Acquisition of Pacific Ventures, Inc."

When she finished, she stared at the paper clutched in her hand and fell silent as she tried to analyze the significance of what she had just read. She looked up at Marion, and in a voice hardly more than a whisper, she asked, "I don't understand. What does this mean?"

"It means that American Paragon is in the process of acquiring Pacific Ventures. You had no way of knowing that six months ago American Paragon entered into secret negotiations with Pacific Ventures. While these negotiations were being conducted, you were passed over at American Paragon for the new position of sales promotion manager, and you started looking for a new job. When your résumé arrived at Pacific Ventures, it probably went directly to the president and CEO, Jim Tanner."

Jeanne broke in, "It was Ed Garman who wrote to me in response to my letter and résumé. He asked me to come out to San Francisco and spend a few days getting acquainted. When we settled on a date, he sent me a business-class airline ticket. He even met me at the airport. I never met Jim Tanner."

"Ed Garman is Jim Tanner's right-hand man. When Jim Tanner doesn't want to be personally involved, he tells Ed Garman to 'see to it.'"

"See to what?" Jeanne asked indignantly.

Now came the hard part. Marion did not particularly like Jeanne. She had too many issues—her blind ambition and her attitude toward Robert only two among many. But she did not *want* to dislike her. After all, they would soon be family. What Marion had to tell Jeanne would hurt, but it was important that she know and understand what she had gotten herself into.

"I'm afraid, Jeanne, that you have been sorely used by Pacific Ventures. The negotiations were dragging on, and when you entered the picture, they saw an opportunity. Their only interest was to get information from you about American Paragon to use in the bargaining process. They anesthetized you with promises of a position in management and then picked your brain! They intellectually violated you, and you were so eager that you didn't see it happening. When you call to accept the position, Ed Garman will not be available to take your call. There's no position waiting for you. It was all a sham!"

Jeanne's face hardened. The color drained out. The thin lines that were her lips tightened, and the words that she forced out between them were metallic, razor-sharp. "I don't believe you! You're a lying bitch, and you made all this up to please Max. He never liked me. He doesn't want me to take his darling son away from him. Well, I am going to San Francisco, and I'm going to take Robert with me."

Marion was unmoved. She had anticipated an outburst. She looked at her watch and saw that with the time difference in San Francisco, it was still possible to contact Pacific Ventures. She opened her handbag, took out her cell phone, and dialed their number. The phone was answered with, "Pacific Ventures, good afternoon."

"Mr. Garman please."

"I'll connect you with his secretary."

"Mr. Garman's office."

"One moment for Mrs. Jeanne Porter," she said and handed the phone to Jeanne.

Jeanne grabbed the phone from Marion's hand. "Hello, Ed?"

"Oh, I'm sorry, Mrs. Porter," the secretary replied. "Mr. Garman is out of town. Is there something I can help you with?"

"When will Mr. Garman return?" she snapped. Jeanne tried not to show it, but she was shaken.

Mr. Garman's secretary was well coached. "Not for two weeks, Mrs. Porter. He's visiting our branch offices. His trip will cover five states. He'll be calling in though. Would you like to leave a message?"

"Yes, tell Mr. Garman that I've decided to accept the position he offered me."

"I'll relay that message to him. I'm certain he'll call you as soon as he can." Jeanne rang off and handed the phone back to Marion.

Marion said nothing, asked no questions she waited for Jeanne to react. And react she did! She glared at Marion and snarled, "You think it's all over, don't you? Well, it's not! When Ed gets my message, he'll call, and then you'll see how fast Robert and I will be off to San Francisco!"

"Don't delude yourself, Jeanne. He won't call. In a few days you will receive a letter full of apologies and reasons why the position is no longer available."

Jeanne was adamant. "You don't know that any more than you know what happened in San Francisco. You weren't there. How could you know?"

"I know because that's how things are done in senior management. Tanner and Garman are trained by experience to seize every opportunity that will benefit them. When your résumé hit Tanner's desk, he could interpret it in two ways. It was either a crude attempt to infiltrate their ranks, which they discounted since you were too low on the executive scale to be a very effective spy, or you knew nothing about the impending merger and were honestly looking to move to another company at a higher level. Either way you were ripe for picking. If what they learned wasn't worth anything to them, all they lost was an airline ticket, a meal or two, and a hotel room, all tax deductible."

Jeanne would have none of it. "It's all a pack of lies. You're out to get me because Max doesn't want Robert to move with me to San Francisco."

Poor Jeanne, Marion thought. *Overly ambitious, ill-prepared, sick Jeanne, all alone in an unreal world of her own making until reality crashes down and crushes her beneath the rubble of her self-esteem, and her dream career vanishes.*

"You fool!" Marion exclaimed. "Don't you realize what a position you've put yourself in? You're sacrificing your marriage and your career for a nonexistent job. Once you leave, there is no returning to either your marriage or your job at American Paragon! Now I've said all I intend to say, and I am going to return to the table. I suggest you do the same. But let me warn you. If you do anything to spoil tonight's celebration, I personally will make your life a misery, to say the least!"

Marion headed toward the door. Suddenly she turned and faced Jeanne, "The Iron Maiden, as you call me, can be your worst enemy, or she can be your best friend. The choice is yours." Marion walked out of the ladies' lounge, leaving Jeanne sitting at the vanity exactly as she had found her.

chapter 31

IT WAS WELL PAST MIDNIGHT when Marion and Max arrived back at Amberfields. As they parted at Marion's door, she reminded Max that they were having brunch with Edna and Arthur Canfield in the morning. They kissed and went their separate ways.

Max arrived at Marion's apartment early the following morning. They had an hour before meeting the Canfields. Marion made coffee, and they leisurely passed the time revisiting the events of last night's dinner.

"With all the trouble Jeanne has caused, I'm still grateful to her," Max reported.

Marion was surprised. "Whatever for? She engineered your exile to Amberfields and stranded you on an ice floe."

"Exactly. That's why I'm grateful. If she hadn't had her agenda, I'd still be living in my house, happy but alone, loving only memories. I'd never have met you. Now I have you to love, and it's all because Jeanne had an agenda."

Marion was astonished. Only her Maxfield Porter, her prince of Amberfields, could find some good in even the most trying situation.

Max was also pleased with the way things had worked out at last night's dinner. "I can't believe how agreeable Jeanne was after coming back from the ladies' lounge. I don't know what you said to placate her, but whatever it was, she returned to the table a changed person."

Marion put her coffee cup down and looked at Max's beaming face. "I wouldn't be too sure about that. She may have seemed agreeable, but it was only on the surface. Jeanne is a very good actress. Underneath she was seething."

Max's expression changed to one of concern. "Do you really think she'll cause trouble?"

"She's a very disturbed girl, darling, in need of professional help. Without it she's capable of anything."

"Does Robert know?"

"He must know. He told us last night about her refusal to accept his promotion and her belief that he would follow her because it would be good for *their* future. She repeated it to me in the ladies' room. She's not acting rationally." A distressing thought flashed into Marion's mind— the women Max and Robert loved both harboring demons.

Max was upset but tried not to show it. "What drives people like that? Doesn't she realize she has obligations to her marriage as well as to her career?"

"She's driven by ambition. She doesn't see herself as she is but as the upper-level executive she wants to be. She's convinced that the job in San Francisco is her golden opportunity. She's going to take it, even though it doesn't exist."

Surprised, Max asked, "What do you mean the job doesn't exist?"

Marion told him about how Jeanne had been conned in San Francisco and her reaction to Marion's warning last night.

"It's hard to believe. Jeanne seems like such a bright girl." Max thought for a moment and then asked, "Why didn't you tell me about this last night on the way back to Amberfields?"

Marion smiled and took Max's hand in hers. "Because, darling, you looked so content with the way things seemed to have worked out, I didn't want to spoil it for you. And I needed time to think how I might soften the blow when Jeanne gets the letter."

"What letter?" Max asked.

"The one she will receive within the next few days from Ed Garman of Pacific Ventures telling her in very apologetic terms that the position they discussed is no longer available. I don't think Jeanne will take it calmly."

"We'll have to tell Robert about this so he'll know what to expect."

"Why don't you call him at his office while I wash out the coffeepot and tidy up the kitchen?"

Max was reluctant. "I'd prefer you to be on the phone. Robert will ask questions I won't be able to answer. I'll use the phone in the living room, and you pick up the kitchen phone. We'll have a three-way conversation, and you can fill in the details."

Max punched in Robert's number and was finally connected. "Hi, Robert, Marion is on the extension, and she has something she wants to pass along to you. Hold on. Ready, honey?"

Marion's voice came on. "Hello, Robert. There's something you should know. There's no job waiting for Jeanne in San Francisco. It was all a ruse to get her to give them information about American Paragon. In a few days a letter will come telling her that the job is no longer available. There's no telling how Jeanne will react when she reads the letter. We wanted you to be forewarned."

"Thanks for the warning, but Jeanne won't be here to receive the letter. We had it out last night. I finally convinced her that I would never leave my job to go with her. She didn't take it too well. After she threw a tantrum, she packed a bag and stormed out. She's probably on a flight to San Francisco by now."

Max spoke up, "There's nothing there for her except disappointment and embarrassment."

"Do you think she will come back?" Marion asked.

"I don't know, Marion. I'd like her to."

"I think she will. But she'll need counseling to overcome her problem."

"Would you help her, Marion?"

"Of course I will, Robert, if she'll let me. She's family."

chapter 32

THE WEDNESDAY, FRIDAY, AND SUNDAY brunch buffets at Amberfields were very popular affairs.. Reservations were required, and Edna Canfield had reserved her usual table for four. In the center of the dining room a number of tables had been moved together to form a large, rectangular stage humorously dubbed the "groaning board" because of the quantity and diversity of the fare it held. The groaning board was circumnavigated by an almost endless line of enthusiastic diners.

The Canfields were seated, nursing their morning cups of coffee while waiting for Marion and Max to arrive. Arthur was reflecting on their coming nuptials. "They've only just met," he commented. "It seems a little abrupt to me. These things should be given time to mature."

Edna looked across the table at Arthur, who had assumed a pontifical air. "Arthur, my darling, please tell me how long we were engaged before we finally got around to setting the date."

"Why, it was three years, my love."

"Exactly, three years. And how old were we when we became engaged?"

Arthur wandered down memory lane. "Let me see now. You were seventeen ... and so lovely, and I was ... twenty-two."

"That's correct, Arthur, and that would have made me twenty and you twenty-five when we married after our three-year engagement. With our whole life before us, three years was not unreasonable. But Max is sixty-nine, and Marion is, I believe, sixty-four. Would you consider a three-year engagement reasonable for them?"

"I see your point, my love. We had time for those three years."

"At their age three years would be an eternity. I'm surprised they have waited this long," Edna said as Marion and Max came through the restaurant entrance and headed for the Canfield's table.

Arthur hailed a greeting, "Welcome, the newlyweds!"

"Not until Sunday, Arthur," Max said and laughed. "Until then we're addressed as the engaged couple."

"The engaged couple," Arthur repeated. "That's extraordinary. Edna and I were just discussing our engagement."

"Arthur likes to reminisce," Edna interjected. Hoping to draw Arthur away from the subject, she said, "Why don't we make our first trip around the buffet?"

"First trip," Arthur said excitedly. "That sounds encouraging."

"Only if you control yourself, Arthur. Remember your cholesterol!"

They joined the line circling the buffet and made their selections. When they returned to the table, Edna surveyed Arthur's plate and removed the prohibited items that he had managed to hide under a layer of fresh fruit. "Arthur, I'm surprised at you," she admonished.

Arthur shrugged his shoulders, and with a sheepish grin, he said, "Nothing ventured—"

Edna turned to Marion and asked, "How are the plans for your wedding coming along?"

"Everything is set," Marion told her. "Momma Maria promises she'll outdo herself, and if the lunch I had there is any indication, it will be a memorable feast."

Max spoke up, "And Arthur, we may be able to share a piece of angel food cake."

"Lovely," Arthur replied, remembering the last lunch they'd had together. "I'm so looking forward to it."

"Since it's a special occasion, Arthur, dear, I think we can dispense with your diet ... for just one day."

The look of anticipation on Arthur's face was almost beatific. "Thank you, my love. I shall be indebted to you forever."

With Arthur's dietary reprieve settled, Edna asked, "Are you planning a long honeymoon?"

"Not right away," Marion responded. "We have some important business to attend to first."

Max saw the quizzical look on Edna's face and spoke up. "Go ahead and tell them, honey."

"First off, we have to settle Max into my apartment. Then we're going to look for a house near Max's old neighborhood. When we find the right one, we'll put both apartments up for sale and move back to the city."

Arthur asked, "Why go back to Summit City? Why not take one of the houses here at Amberfields? You're eligible, or you will be after Sunday."

"As nice as Amberfields is, moving back to the city is something Max and I want to do."

"But Amberfields has everything one could possibly want," Arthur insisted. "You seem so happy here."

Edna knew that what was drawing Max back to the city was much deeper than what Amberfields had to offer. It was what Amberfields could not offer him. "Arthur, my love, some people need more than a golf course and a clubhouse to be fulfilled."

Arthur thought for a moment. "Oh, yes, I see it now. I was casting Max in my mold. I have you, my love, and the golf course and the clubhouse. I need very little more. I'm really an uncomplicated person."

"I know, darling," Edna said, reaching across the table and taking Arthur's hand in hers. "And that's what I love about you."

Edna turned and addressed Max. "You were never really comfortable here at Amberfields. Is that the reason you want to go back to the city?"

Max thought before he answered. He knew how Edna felt about living at Amberfields, and he didn't want to offend her. "That's part of it. I could see why people enjoyed living here, but it wasn't for me. I saw myself slipping into routines that were to me unchallenging and unfulfilling. I was used to a fuller, more active life on a broader stage. I couldn't change."

"But you did change," Edna insisted.

"Yes, I did," Max admitted. "Meeting Marion changed a lot of things. For one thing I started being myself again. When I came to Amberfields, I didn't think there was a chance of my ever returning to Summit City. My house was gone, and most of my belongings were sold or put into storage to be disposed of later. I even resisted going back to the city to visit my old friends because it would be too painful to leave again and return to my lonely apartment. I found it difficult to accept the changes that came with my move to Amberfields."

Max paused, and Marion took over the telling. "Max and I have so much in common. It didn't take long for us to find out that we liked the same things. Classic motion pictures, for example. I'm a film nut. I love classic films, the ones they made in the thirties and forties with stars like Gable and Crawford. I'd catch them on PBS every Saturday night. Later when I got cable, I watched them almost every night on TCM. Within five minutes of meeting Max I learned that he was a film collector, that he had a collection of over three hundred films all packed away in storage because there was no place for them at Amberfields. He no longer had his house with the theater in the basement, so there were no shows for the neighborhood kids or the senior citizen groups or the college students in the communication and arts courses. That was the reason for collecting—to share them with people who loved them and learned from them."

Edna now understood the immediate attraction these two people had for one another. When Max had breakfast with her and told her how uncomfortable and out of place he felt at Amberfields, she thought it was a natural reaction to being abruptly torn away from all that was familiar. She thought he would overcome these feelings as he settled into the routine of Amberfields. Now she realized that no routine could have cured what he felt! That is, until he met Marion. He was no longer without purpose. He had found his soul mate. Edna had been right in one thing. Theirs was a love affair destined to happen.

"It was all worth it," Max said. "If I hadn't allowed myself to be talked into coming to Amberfields, I never would have met Marion. You can call it kismet or destiny or say that it was written in the stars. All I know is that even against my better judgment, coming to Amberfields was the smartest move I ever made!

"Now I'm ready for another turn around the buffet table. Anyone coming with me?" Arthur was the first to rise to the invitation.

chapter 33

IT WAS 1:30 WHEN THEY left the Canfields. Max asked, "What would you like to do this afternoon?"

Marion needed no time to think about it. "It's such a lovely day. We should do something outside. How about walking down to the lake and you teaching me how to skip stones? Just give me a few minutes to change into something more appropriate for stone-throwing." Ten minutes later they walked arm in arm toward the lake. Giant cotton balls of cumulous clouds drifted slowly by, accentuating the blue of the sky. The temperature, if they had bothered to notice, was neither too hot nor too cool. It was a perfect day for lovers.

Max walked with his head lowered slightly, his eyes scanning the ground for stones. When he spotted one that looked promising, he uncoupled himself from Marion's arm, stooped, picked it up, and inspected it carefully. Just any old stone wouldn't do. It had to be the right size and shape. If he was satisfied that it fulfilled the stringent requirements, he put it in his jacket pocket. He repeated this ritual until his pocket bulged with stones.

"These stones are perfect for skipping," he told Marion as they continued toward the lake. He held one up to illustrate. "They have to be thin but not too thin. They need some weight but not too much, and they have to be as flat on one side as possible."

Marion took the stone from him, held it up, and examined it. She rotated it between her fingers and then let it fall onto her palm and hefted it. "And you're going to make this stone bounce across the water like a rubber ball?" she said with apparent skepticism. "That seems like a lot to expect from a stone."

"My dear woman," he said with mock indignation, "skip, not bounce. I would have you know that I trained for years to perfect the art of skipping stones. With training, you, too, will become an expert skipper. Even though it may take a number of years to accomplish, I will dedicate myself to the task. Now if you will accompany me to the lake, I will demonstrate the art of skipping stones across water." He presented his arm to Marion. She hooked her arm through his, and they strode off to the water's edge.

The lake was perfectly smooth. There was no breeze to ruffle the surface, and the water fowl were on the far side, out of the way. Max took a stone from his pocket.

"Everything is A-OK for a perfect skip," he assured Marion.

"I wait with bated breath," she responded.

Marion watched as Max took his position at the lake's edge and did a little jig with his feet to set them firmly. Then when he was satisfied with his stance, he began to flap his arms about. He glanced over to Marion to see if she was taking in his performance. "Just warming up," he assured her. She knew he was clowning for her benefit, and she loved every minute of it.

"Honey," he exclaimed over his shoulder, "you are about to see a stone hop, skip, and jump but not bounce across the water."

Max spun around. His arm whipped out, and the stone shot forward a few inches above the water, came down, touched the surface, immediately became airborne again, and skipped twice more before it sank.

"That's marvelous!" Marion exclaimed, adding applause for effect.

Max, who never needed the response of an audience, reveled in Marion's. He took out another stone, wound up, and flung it out across the water. This time the stone skipped four times before it disappeared into the lake.

"Bravo!" Marion called out. "That was farther than the first."

Max turned to face Marion. "Now it's time for your first lesson."

He took another stone from his pocket. "Now watch as I position the stone in my throwing hand." He grasped the flat stone between his thumb and middle finger with his index finger held firmly against the edge. He rotated his hand so Marion could see the position of the stone from different angles.

After she took the stone from Max, she tried to place it as he had shown her. She had difficulty getting her index finger along the edge of the stone. Max recognized the problem. The stone was too large for her small hand. He rummaged in his pocket and produced a smaller stone.

"Here, try this one," he said, and they exchanged stones.

The new stone fit her hand, and she positioned it carefully, held out her hand, and rotated it for Max's approval.

"That's perfect. You'll make a great skipper."

"Can I throw it now?"

"Not yet. You've only learned to hold the stone. Now you have to learn how to throw it so it will skip and not dive under the water. Watch me as I go through the motions. I'll do it in slow motion so you can follow along."

Translating the dynamic moves of the pitch into slow motion produced an eccentric pantomime that elicited peals of laughter from Marion. Max stopped his demonstration in the middle of the pitch and turned to Marion. "What's so funny?" he asked.

"It's the slow motion," Marion replied, still laughing. "It reminded me of an old silent comedy. I envisioned a custard pie in your hand instead of a stone and another pie coming into the frame and hitting you in the face."

Max saw the humor of the scene Marion had painted, and he joined in her laughter. When their laughter subsided, Max asked, "Now how am I going to teach you how to skip stones if you interject scenes from old silent comedies? Skipping stones is very serious stuff."

"Okay, no more old silent comedies," Marion replied. "I'll concentrate on your demonstration. But how about demonstrating it in real time? Surprisingly, slow motion is hard to follow."

"All right. I'll go through each move separately with a verbal explanation of what I'm doing. Then I'll skip a stone so you can see the whole sequence in action."

"Sounds like a plan. Carry on, professor."

"Are you sure you're ready?"

"Absolutely. I want to skip a stone before the lake dries up."

"Very funny. Now follow me closely."

"To the ends of the earth," she said softly, seriously.

Suddenly the mood changed. Max wanted to take her in his arms and smother her with kisses, but it might prove embarrassing. Out in the open, they were in sight of anyone at Amberfields who cared to look at them. Instead he took her hand, raised it to his lips, and kissed it. She kissed the index finger of her other hand and put it to Max's lips. They were one moment closer to achieving what they both wanted.

Max came back to the business of skipping stones. He showed her the stance and the importance of "digging in" her feet so she wouldn't lose her balance, of "winding the spring," pivoting the upper body around at the hips, and "releasing the spring" with the sidearm pitch so the stone would leap off upon the proper trajectory.

Marion followed closely. "I'm ready," she reported. "Let me throw one."

Max complied and stepped back to give her room. Marion positioned the stone in her hand, set her feet firmly on the bank, brought her arm back, and swiveled around, "winding the spring." *So far so good*, Max thought. She "released the spring" and spun forward. Her arm came around, and the stone took off, arched up into a high trajectory, and splashed into the lake. "What did I do wrong?" she wanted to know.

"Nothing that can't be fixed," he assured her. "First you threw overhand. Secondly when you released the stone, you let go with all three fingers. As you throw your arm forward, open your thumb and middle finger and let the stone roll off the index finger, causing it to spin. The sidearm pitch adds the power. The secret is to keep your arm straight at the elbow and never bring your hand above your waist."

"I think I get it now," Marion exclaimed. "Let me try it again."

"Okay, pick a stone and get set. I'll guide you through the sidearm pitch."

Marion, concentrating on setting up her pitch, didn't see Max move behind her. As she started her swivel to "wind the spring," Max, from behind, placed his left arm around her waist and wrapped his right hand around her right wrist with the intention of guiding her through the sidearm pitch. He felt Marion's body stiffen and recoil in horror. The memory of the night Carl had grabbed her from behind and thrown her on the bed exploded into the here and now. She screamed and tore away from Max. Still screaming, she turned to face him, her fists pounding against his chest.

Max was dumbstruck. He started to wrap his arms around her, to pull her tightly against him, but he realized intuitively that it would be the wrong thing to do. He let her pull away.

"Marion, darling," he gasped, "what's wrong?"

"It's no good! I thought you were different, but you're the same as all the rest!" She wailed and exploded into a fountain of tears.

"Please, Marion," he pleaded. "Tell me what happened! I don't understand!"

"I thought I was free," she gasped between sobs. "But she told me it would happen again, and it has. It will always happen to me. I can hear her taunting me, sneering at me, 'I told you! I told you! I told you!!' Now I know I can never give my love to anyone. The price is too high!"

Max was confused. Marion wasn't making sense. "Who is she," he asked, "and what did she tell you?" Then it came to him. "Is she your demon?"

"Yes!" Marion wailed. "And I'll never be free of her!"

"Marion, I love you. Please let me help you," he begged.

"Help me?" she cried. "You can't help me! No one can help me!"

In desperation Max pleaded, "I'm the man who loves you. Doesn't that mean anything?"

"It must be so easy for you to say those pretty things. They always sound as though they're being said for the first time. But they're just words. When he got tired of the words, Carl didn't even bother to ask. He just took what he wanted! You're a man. You'll do the same."

Max knew that any denial would fall on deaf ears. This was a different Marion, a Marion he didn't know. Bewildered, he stood there, unable to react. He watched as she turned from him, and crying hysterically, she ran back to her apartment. The sound of her crying echoed in his ears long after she had gone.

Max looked out across the lake. The sun was still shining. The temperature was still delightful. The geese and ducks were still paddled around in circles, and on the links golfers pursued their passion. It was the perfect setting for the perfect day he had promised Marion. Now he stood alone at the edge of the lake, his heart ripped out by what had happened and the frustration of not being able to help her.

"I should have known better than to fall in love at my age! Love is for kids!" He reached into his pocket and removed a stone and threw it at the lake. Instead of skipping, it dived under the surface and sank to the bottom. He took the remaining stones from his pocket, held them out over the lake, and let them fall through his fingers to splash into the water. He watched them sink and then turned and trudged back to his ice floe.

chapter 34

WHAT HAD STARTED AS ANOTHER perfect day with Marion had turned into a disaster! Back in his apartment, Max racked his brain for anything he might have said or done to cause Marion's hysteria. Everything had happened so suddenly. He could recall only fragments of what she had said. But he did remember one thing because it was so frightening he could still feel it stabbing at his heart. *Now I know I can never give my love to anyone. The price is too high!*

Max picked up the phone, speed-dialed Marion's number, and got her voice mail. Too upset to talk to a machine, he hung up and raced to her apartment. There was no answer to his knock. He wanted to call out to her through the door, but thought better of it. Why advertise their struggle to her neighbors? If she was inside, it was evident she didn't want to see or talk to him. Frustrated, he returned to his apartment, got his car keys, and blindly drove to Summit City and Cinemabilia.

Dave Benjamin knew something was wrong as soon as Max walked in. Distress was written all over him. It was in the absence of his customary cheerful entrance to the shop, in the way he stood listlessly thumbing through a box of old photos, but mostly in his eyes. And it was what he saw in Max's eyes that concerned Dave the most.

They had been friends for a long time. They shared a common

interest in film, and it was at Max's suggestion that Dave had started Cinemabilia. Now Dave knew that he must ferret out his friend's problem and try to help him. He owed Max that and much more. He knew instinctively it had to do with Marion.

"What brings you back to our fair city?"

"I was just passing. Thought I'd stop in and say hello and see how thing are going."

"Things are fine. How about you? Is everything still okay at Amberfields?"

Max didn't answer immediately. He took a photo out of a box and examined it without seeing it. Finally he slipped the photo back into the box, turned to face Dave, and said, "Not okay. In fact, pretty damned awful!"

Dave ticked off, "Drafty apartment, noisy neighbors, or maybe nosey neighbors? Any one of which would make the place pretty damned awful. Want to talk about it?"

"Why?" Max spat out the word, making his answer more defiant than questioning. "Will talking change it or make it go away?"

"Possibly, even probably," Dave replied, "but for setting your thinking straight, absolutely! Since you are reluctant to discuss your problem with an old and true friend, namely me, I am forced to take the initiative. Do you think I could stand by and watch you, my best friend, throw in the towel without trying to help you?"

"Please, Dave, it won't do any good."

Dave was indignant. "Please my sore feet! Did Sweet Leilani walk out on you? Is that what this is all about?"

Max was taken aback. He shouted, "What do you know about it? Who told you?"

"You did. You came in here looking lower than a rattler's belly. It doesn't take an advanced degree in psychology to know something is amiss with you and your lady love. You're covered in black crepe, looking for help but not wanting to talk about it. So I'll tell you what we're going to do. I'm going to close up, and we'll go back to my apartment, where you are going to tell me all about it."

In his apartment, Dave saw Max seated and then headed to the kitchen to brew a pot of coffee. While Dave fussed with the coffeemaker,

Max fidgeted in the chair and finally got up, walked into the kitchen, and sat down at the kitchen table.

"I must have been an old fool, falling in love at my age. Love is a young man's game, isn't it?"

Before he answered, Dave finished measuring the coffee into the filter and pressed the start button. His actions were slow and deliberate, giving him time to weigh his answer.

"No man's a fool to love someone. I'm certain that if Dorothy were alive, you would still be very much in love with her, and she with you. I don't think love has an age limit."

Max found no fault with what Dave said, especially the part about Dorothy. The Canfields also came to mind. But Dorothy was gone, now just a memory. And now Marion too was gone, and he was left with only memories to love.

Max looked up at Dave. "I know you're right, Dave, but I'd feel better if I knew what caused her to break like that. One minute we're happily skipping stones across the lake, and the next she was hysterical. I keep searching my memory for anything I might have said or done, but it's all a blur."

"You'll remember, Max. Just keep talking, and it will all come back to you."

"I'm not sure I want to remember. Maybe I should be trying to forget."

Dave was leaning against the counter when the coffeemaker signaled that the coffee was ready. He took two mugs down from the cabinet, filled them, and placed one in front of Max. Against Max's refusal, Dave took a bottle of brandy from the cupboard and poured a tot into Max's mug. "Drink up, Max. You've got a hard ride ahead of you."

Max looked up. "That sounds like a line from one of your horse operas."

"It's just my way of telling you that it's not going to be easy, whichever way you choose. But it seems to me that trying to find out what caused this explosion so it can be corrected and I can dance at your wedding is a lot better than going off in a corner and being miserable for the rest of your life."

Max slowly shook his head and smiled. "You know, Dave, you're a pretty smart guy for a cowboy from the Bronx."

"Thanks. You're pretty smart yourself ... for an old fool. What were you doing when Marion blew up? What were you talking about?"

"I was teaching her to skip stones. She seemed eager to learn. I believe she thought it would please me if she learned. She was like that."

"How was she doing?"

"She was doing fine until she pitched the stone. She had trouble with the sidearm pitch. She threw overhand, and the stone sank when it hit the water."

"Was that when she got hysterical?"

"No, she wanted to try again. I demonstrated the sidearm pitch and explained why it was important. She took another stone and positioned herself and reared back to throw. I saw that her arm was too high, and she was going to throw overhand again. If she threw the stone like that, it would certainly sink as soon as it hit the water, and I didn't want her to be discouraged by another failure. I stepped behind her, put my left arm around her waist, and grasped her wrist with my right hand so I could guide her arm through the pitch."

Dave became excited. "You came up from behind and grabbed her?"

"Yes, but don't make it sound so ominous. I didn't grab her! I was just trying to help her."

"Maybe she didn't know that."

Dave became meditative for a while. Then softly he said, "It sounds like she's been manhandled before, and your grabbing her from behind brought it all back. She may have been living with it for a long time."

Dave wasn't sure he should go any further. This didn't sound like a job for an armchair psychologist. Just as he was about to tell Max that Marion might benefit from professional help, Max exclaimed, "Her demon! I remember now. She said it was her demon!"

"What demon?" Dave was intrigued.

"When I asked her to marry me, she told me she wanted to but couldn't until she got rid of her demon. I offered to help her, but she said she had to do it herself. I tried to get her to tell me more about the demon, but she never gave me any details except to tell me that since we met, she was certain she could defeat it."

"Did she mention the demon after you grabbed her?"

"She referred to a voice that kept saying, 'I told you! I told you!' That could only have been the demon speaking. She was hysterical at the time and said a lot of things that jumbled up in my mind. I was in shock. I'm still trying to sort them out."

"Can you remember anything at all?"

"I do remember one thing she said because it was so ominous. She said, 'Now I know I can never give my love to anyone. The price is too high!' I can't let her believe that. I've got to show her it isn't true."

"How do you propose to do that?" Dave asked. "You realize she has a problem, possibly a serious one that may require professional help. Face it, Max. Loving her is not enough!"

Max hesitated before he answered. Then in a slow and determined voice from deep within, he said, "I know, but it's a start, and it's as much for me as it is for her. She saved me from drifting away into a gray existence. Without her, I'll be back on that damn ice floe, cold and lonely and miserable."

The significance of *Nanook of the North* now became apparent to Dave. "Feel like talking about it?" he asked again.

Max realized that now he did feel like talking about it. He told Dave about his dislike of Amberfields and why he had agreed to settle there, about how he and Marion had met in the mail room and how paradise and the ice floe had come about and the meaning of the two videos. It was early evening when he finished.

Max got up from the table. "I'd better get back."

"Why?"

"You know why. I've got to talk to her. Maybe she'll pick up the phone or answer the door."

Dave shook his head. "Bad idea, Max. Give her a little time to get over the shock she's had. Sleep here tonight. You can head back tomorrow."

Max brought out his cell phone. "I'm going to call her. If she's there, maybe she'll answer the phone."

"Don't do it, Max. Tonight you're the bad guy. After she's had time to think about what happened and remembers who and what you really are, things may be different."

Max snapped the cover over the phone and slid it back into his pocket. "Sure, Dave, tomorrow things might be different, but I'll still have to get through tonight! I doubt I'll be able to sleep. There's too much going on in my head. I keep wondering what I'm going to do tomorrow."

"Tomorrow will take care of itself if you let it. Stop worrying now about what you're going to do tomorrow. In the light of day Marion may decide that she needs you to help defeat her demon. You two are crazy in love, and that leads me to conclude that you need each other to solve this problem. Now I'm going to mix up a nightcap. It'll help you to sleep."

For the first time since Marion's outburst Max smiled. *Friends come in all shapes and sizes*, he thought, *but none better than Dave Benjamin, AKA Lone Star.*

The two friends sat in Dave's study, silently nursing their nightcaps before turning in. Dave looked at Max over the rim of his brandy glass. The pained look had returned to Max's face. Before he had chance to say anything that might shake him out of his distress, Max turned to him, and in a voice fraught with pain he said, "I don't know what I'd do if I lost Marion. When Dorothy died, I suffered her death and felt I would never get over her loss. But time works wonders on the mind, and I soon realized that she was gone and could never return. Yet she left me with such wonderful memories of our life together that I hadn't really lost her. I had closure, and my life went on.

"But with Marion it's different. She's very much alive yet lost to me. We'll be living in close proximity to one another. We'll see each other in the mail room, in the dining room, and in a hundred other places in the Amberfields community. How does one get over that? To be so close and yet so far apart? There could never be any closure. I'll never be able to live with that. It's the kind of living hell that tears one apart!"

"Max, if Marion loves you as much as you love her, then she's also having one hell of a night. She'll have had time to weigh the good against the perceived bad, your alleged motives against her reactions, and since she's a pretty clever woman, she'll reconsider yesterday's events in a more reasonable light."

"Sure, Dave, like you said, tomorrow things will be different. I'll see to that."

chapter 35

SOMEHOW MARION FOUND HER WAY back to her apartment. She fumbled with her key and flung the door open. Once inside she staggered into the bedroom and fell onto the bed. She buried her head in her pillow and wept hysterically. The phone rang, but she was in no condition to answer. Anyway, it was probably Max, she thought, and she could not talk to him. She could never talk to him again. The phone continued to ring, but getting no response, it went to her voice mail.

She didn't hear the knock on her door and wouldn't have answered it if she had. She wept for a long time. Gradually the weeping turned to sobs, and as twilight dimmed the room, the sobbing stopped. Exhausted, brokenhearted, Marion lay wondering why she had allowed this to happen. Once again she had been betrayed by the man she loved. The voice had been right. All men were the same. They only took, never gave. But if that were true, why had Max made her so happy? Certainly Max had given from the moment they met, and the ring was tangible proof of that. Had it all been a plot to trap her? She was very confused.

"Everything he did, he did to make me happy," she said aloud. The sound of her own voice surprised her. At first she thought it was the demon speaking. But why would the demon say anything complimentary about Max? Then she recognized the voice as her own. Her confusion deepened.

"Yet it ended the way the voice told me it would, with Max attacking me just as Carl did!" This admission unleashed another flood of weeping. "Oh, why did I have to fall in love again?" she moaned as tears cascaded down her cheeks.

By the time Marion had cried herself into exhaustion, the room was dark. The darkness pressed in on her. Her head began spinning, and a wave of nausea overtook her. She groped for the bedside lamp and snapped it on. After she slid her legs over the edge of the bed, she sat up with her head bent forward, cradled in her hands. When the vertigo subsided, she slid off the bed and unsteadily made her way to the bathroom. Holding the door jamb to steady herself, she slid her other hand along the wall to the light switch. The light flared, and Marion saw her reflection in the mirror above the sink. What she saw staggered her.

The ravaged face that stared back at her bore little resemblance to the face she had seen when she had gotten up that morning. It was lined and blotched, her eyes red and swollen. Her hair hung in tangled strings. She looked, she thought, ancient and ugly, and it frightened her.

That morning in this same mirror she had seen herself looking at the very least ten years younger than her sixty-four years. Her face was unlined, and her eyes glowed with the anticipation of spending another day with Max. She had spent extra time on her makeup and hair and in picking out just the right clothes to wear. She still had a young woman's figure, firm and perfectly proportioned for her size. She was happy with how she looked. But that was this morning. Now it was all gone, and she doubted it could ever return.

Marion washed her face and ran a comb through her hair. It did little to change her mood. Her thoughts turned to Max. She had loved him. There was no denying that. Reluctantly she admitted she still loved him, and the thought of having lost him immersed her in a sea of loneliness. She yearned for his touch. She held her hand out for Max to take in his and kiss her fingers. But he would never again be there to touch her, to kiss her.

That's ridiculous! You're not a lovesick schoolgirl. It's time you came to your senses. He's gone ... and good riddance. You're better off without him.

The voice was back!

Didn't I tell you it would happen again just like Carl? How many times have I told you that all men are alike?

"Yes, you've told me over and over again," Marion screamed, "but your ranting has done nothing except make me miserable and lonely. What gives you the right to enter my head and mess up my life?"

You did, Marion. Carl died because you rejected him. You locked him out, and he died. The moment you assumed the guilt for his death, I was born. I've only been telling you what you wanted to hear.

"Well, I don't want to hear it anymore. Max is gone. I've lost him. After the way I acted, I'm too embarrassed to see him again, all because I believed you."

The voice did not respond. Marion's face hardened. Her nostrils flared, and her eyes glinted. "Now get out of my head," she shouted. "I don't need you anymore. Do you think Max would want a woman who hears voices in her head? You've done your job. You've made me a crazy woman. No sane man would ever want me now."

I've only done what you wanted, Marion. You wanted guilt, so I gave you guilt. As you said, I've done the job you gave me, and there's no longer a need for me. I'm leaving, but I'm not going far. You can't lose me as long as you believe you were responsible for Carl's death, and you'll never forget the charred corpse they made you identify!

Stunned, Marion tried to prevent that terrible memory from projecting itself onto her mind's eye, but the image was too strong.

This is what you are responsible for, Marion. You loved him, and this is what your love led to. This is what called me to you.

Marion could stand no more. She clapped her hands over her ears. Her head began to spin, and as darkness closed in around her, she fell to the floor.

When she regained consciousness, the room was filling with the gray light of dawn. She was lying half in her bedroom and half in the bathroom, where she had fallen when she had fainted. She was racked with pain in her body and head. She managed to sit up, bracing her back against the bathroom doorjamb. She sat that way for a long time, thinking about yesterday. She remembered screaming when Max grabbed her and running away from him. She remembered returning to her apartment and crying herself into oblivion ... and seeing a stranger's haggard face in the mirror. But she remembered little else. Now it was morning, and she had to do something to let Max know that it was all over between them. Actually she didn't know why she had to do it. Everything was a jumble. Slowly little bits and pieces came into focus.

Marion lifted herself from the floor and turned on the shower. She threw off her clothes and let the spray wash away the cobwebs in her head and the pain from her body. The water washed over her, cascading down her breasts, racing between them as a river through a chasm. As she washed, she felt the firmness of her body. She knew she would have gladly given herself to Max had he asked. Now they would never know the pleasure of sharing each other.

When she got out of the shower, she felt better physically, but she couldn't shake the crushing sadness. Bits of the night before rose to the surface of her memory. She started to remember the voice returning and some of the things it had said. Why had it claimed that she had called it to her? The more she remembered, the more confused she became. Was Max as devious and self-serving as the voice pictured him? Or could his grabbing her have been an accident that triggered the memory of her rape? She couldn't answer either question. She knew which one she wanted to be true. But suppose it was the other? She couldn't take the chance. It might kill her.

Marion dried and combed her hair. Outwardly she was beginning to look more like herself. Inside she was still shattered. She dressed in a pair of satin lounging pajamas, made a cup of strong black coffee, went to her dressing table, and took out the ring box. She sat down at her desk, took out a pen and paper, and began to write.

"My Darling Max—"

chapter 36

A T THE SOUND OF HIS door chime Max put his coffee cup down and rose to see who it was. He wanted it to be Marion but knew the chance of that was slight. "Who is it?" he growled at the door.

"It's Charlie from the mail room, Mr. Porter. I have a package for you."

Cautiously Max opened the door and was greeted by the mail room clerk. "Good morning, Mr. Porter. It's going to be another great day today. Weather-wise, that is," he exclaimed as he held forth a heavily taped manila envelope. "Mrs. Wade asked me to deliver it to you. She said she didn't want it put in your box."

Max took the package. "Charlie, do you know where Mrs. Wade is now?"

"Sure, Mr. Porter, she's in her apartment. She called the mail room and asked me to come up and get the package. I got it and came right up here."

"Thanks, Charlie." Max reached into his pocket, pulled out a five-dollar bill, and handed it to Charlie.

"Oh, gee, Mr. Porter, you don't have to do that. Mrs. Wade already paid for the delivery."

"That's okay, Charlie. It's for the information."

Max raced back to the kitchenette and ripped open the envelope.

The little velour-covered ring box fell into his hand. There was also a letter.

Max pondered the short love affair they had shared. It was nothing more than an attraction that had started in the mail room and blossomed into love when he wrote a simple letter to go with two videos. Now he wondered if the love affair had ended with another letter. With unsteady hands he opened the envelope and read the letter.

My Darling Max,

I deluded myself into thinking I had conquered my demon simply because I no longer heard its voice. I deceived you and myself when I told you I was ready to marry you.

The memory of what Carl did to me and the guilt I bear for what I did to him make it impossible for us to have a life together. What happened at the lake could and probably would happen again. I love you, but I'd rather lose you than inflict my demon on you. The last thing you need in your life is a crazy woman.

Darling, you are still one of the good guys, and I don't know how I will live without you.

Sadly,

Marion

Max dropped the letter and ring box into his pocket and raced to Marion's apartment. There was no answer to his ringing or knocking, yet he sensed her presence within. "Marion," he called out, "open this door, or I'll break it down!"

Her answer came through the door. "Please, Max. Go away. There's nothing more to talk about. I said it all in the letter."

"Marion, I have your letter with me. If you don't open the door, I'll call security and read them the last sentence of the letter, which could be construed as a final farewell. You know what a scene that will cause."

"You wouldn't dare! Would you?"

"You bet I would! Don't think I'm going to give you up without a fight. You and I are going to have a face-to-face talk, and I mean now!"

Reluctantly Marion unlocked the door and opened it but kept the security chain in place. Max was still on the outside.

"All the way, Marion. We can't solve anything here in the hallway. We're disturbing the neighbors. You don't want that any more than I do."

"Max, I'm not dressed. I just got up. I'm a mess."

"That's okay. It's the way I'm going to see you every morning for the rest of our lives. I'm no Adonis first thing in the morning either. Now put on a robe or a dressing gown or a raincoat or a fur coat. Then take this damn chain off and let's sit down and talk."

She relented and slowly slid the chain from its restraint. She stepped back, and Max entered the apartment. Marion was not as badly attired as she had led Max to believe. She had on a quilted robe over green satin pajamas. Her feet were bare. True, her hair wasn't up to its usual perfection, and she wore no makeup; however, to Max she was as beautiful as ever and far from the mess she claimed to be.

He gently held her elbow and guided her to a chair. Then he sat down opposite her. "First, let's get one thing straight. You are not going to lose me! I'm the guy that loves you and is going to marry you in spite of any notion you may have to the contrary. In case you have forgotten, everything is set for our wedding tomorrow, and we mustn't disappoint Momma Maria.

"Secondly I'm the only one who can call you a crazy woman and then only when we're doing something nutty together like skipping stones across the lake.

"Now let's talk about this demon of yours. I want you to tell me everything. Maybe it's something we can work out together. If not, we'll get professional help. Nothing is going to keep us from being together."

Marion was indignant. "You don't understand, Max. You're forcing me to talk about things I'd rather forget. What good does it do to dredge up the horror and shame of my last night with Carl?"

Max was adamant. "I do understand that, honey. But I also understand that the truth is in the telling. Somewhere in the horror of that night lies the answer to why you acquired this demon. I also know that you will never defeat your demon until you bring it out into the open and face it in the light of reason."

The silence was palpable as Marion tried to come to grips with Max's argument. In all the intervening years, she had told no one about that night—not the police woman who came to the house or her doctor or her sister-in-law or her friends. No one must ever know that Carl, the husband whom she had loved all those years, had brutally raped her.

She was still attractive, and as time went by, she had started to date again. But her dates always ended in the same way with an effort to service a widow's sexual requirements. She was continually "hit upon" at work. She had never succumbed, and soon she became known as the Iron Maiden. It only added fodder to that damned voice. *Men are no good*, the voice would scream. *Be careful, be wary, he will be like all men. He will take and give nothing in return.* Marion had begun to believe the voice. She developed a phobia of being touched and had stopped dating altogether.

Then she came to Amberfields where she had met Max and somehow fallen in love. Now, on the eve of what was to have been their wedding day, they were alienated and Max was fighting to drive her demon out into the open to destroy it and to save them.

Max waited tensely for Marion's response. She slowly emerged from her dark memories, looked across at Max, and smiled that radiant smile he so loved. She didn't have to say anything. He knew what her decision was.

She told him about that night, leaving nothing out. At first she felt acutely embarrassed, but Max assured her that her reaction was perfectly normal and that she was able to conquer it. He let her talk at her own pace, only interrupting to ask a question when necessary. He held her hand, squeezing it gently when he felt she needed reinforcement, lifting it to his lips and kissing her fingers during some of the most painful passages. At times his face reddened, not from embarrassment but from anger. He wanted to lash out at the man who had so perversely misused her. But he was long gone, and now Max had to help Marion erase his legacy.

The telling was over. Max was trying to formulate all he had learned into a reasonable explanation of Marion's problem. Surprisingly it was Marion who did the explaining.

"It's a matter of the victim assuming the guilt, isn't it, Max? I felt guilty because I was his wife, and I didn't give in to him. If I had, there would have been no drunken stupor, no rape, and no crash. It was as though I had killed Carl. I really believed it. I wrapped myself up in my guilt and never allowed myself to speak about it to anyone. Only the voice knew. But that's what I still don't understand. Where did the voice come from?"

Max felt he had a plausible explanation. "It was your voice, darling. You hated Carl for what he did to you. You transferred that hate to any man who came close to you, who touched you physically. You made your voice your conscience. Then when we met and fell in love, the memory of that night began to blur. When I unintentionally manhandled you, trying to teach you the sidearm pitch, it revived that horrible memory, and the voice came back to life. I could cut off my arms for being so stupid."

Marion shook her head. "Oh, Max! How could you have known? Besides, I wouldn't like it if you didn't have arms. How would I ever learn the sidearm pitch? How could you put your ring back on my finger or hold me if you didn't have arms?"

"Now that you put it that way, I don't feel so bad. Since I have my arms, how about letting me put them to good use?" He took the ring from his pocket and put it back on her finger. "See, everything works fine."

Marion became pensive. "Max, could it happen again? Could the fear and hate come back?"

"Possibly. All we've done is to define the problem and trace it back to its beginning. With our limited layman's knowledge, that's all we could do, but it was enough to get us together again. The full cure is a little more complicated than love conquers all. The rest will have to be done by a professional."

"By professional you mean a psychiatrist? I don't think I could handle that."

"Oh, sure you can. The hardest part of analysis is finding the root of your problem. You've already done that. The rest ought to be fairly easy. A few sessions with Hal Garfield should set everything straight."

"The casual way you mentioned his name means he's another one of your buddies. He is, isn't he?"

"How did you guess? He's one of my poker buddies and a good friend. He straightened me out after Dorothy's death. I don't know what would have happened if Hal hadn't been there for me."

Marion hesitated for a moment. "He's a real psychiatrist, an MD?" she questioned.

"He's one of the best, darling. They don't get any better."

Marion thought for a moment. "Well, he saved you for me. The least I can do is let him save me for you."

"You don't mind?" Max asked. "Telling it all over again to a stranger?"

"He's your buddy. How could he be a stranger?"

Max's heart raced. Marion was herself again. The resonance had returned. They vibrated as only two people in love could.

"I'm not afraid anymore," she said. "I think your buddy, Hal, will have a pretty easy time of it."

"Don't make it too easy for him. He has a reputation to uphold."

"But you did all the work, darling. Getting me to bare my soul was a big gamble that could have gone terribly wrong. But as soon as I relented and started talking, things became clearer, not distorted by fear or shame. You were right when you said the truth was in the telling."

Marion smiled, and Max saw the luminescence of her eyes. He knew that she was happy and that she would be able to beat the demon.

"Now we have some unfinished business to take care of," she said through the smile. "I didn't give you a chance to finish showing me the sidearm pitch. Would you like to continue the lesson?"

"If you feel up to it, get dressed, and we'll go to the lake and pick up where we left off."

Marion gave him a look of disdain. "And what's wrong with right here and right now?"

It took Max only a heartbeat to get the message. "Nothing," he responded, "absolutely nothing!"

They stood in the center of the room, and she assumed the pitching position. He moved behind her and gently placed his arm around her waist, and with his other hand he took hold of her wrist. "Now keep your arm low and don't forget the follow through," he instructed.

Marion pivoted, and with Max guiding her arm, she threw an imaginary stone with a perfect sidearm pitch. As Max released her hand, she spun around until she was cradled in his arms. Max heard an almost inaudible sigh and recognized it as the demon's death rattle. Marion was finally free. He pulled her tightly to him and whispered, "The voice is gone forever, sweetheart. You'll never have to worry about voices anymore. Tomorrow we'll be Max and Marion Porter just as we were destined to be."

They held each other and felt the warmth caress their bodies. Neither of them had had much sleep the night before, and the strain caught up to them. Max took Marion's hand and led her to the couch. They sat down side by side, and as she had done at Lone Star's apartment while viewing the film, she pulled his arm around her shoulders and laid her head on his chest. They had found their island paradise. As they sat under the swaying palms, they listened to the rhythm of the rolling surf and the strains of "Sweet Leilani" until sleep enveloped them and they dreamed of stones skipping across the Rubicon.

Printed in the United States
By Bookmasters